VIGILANTE

THE VIGILANTE CHRONICLES™ BOOK ONE

NATALIE GREY

MICHAEL ANDERLE

DISRUPTIVE IMAGINATION

VIGILANTE TEAM

Thanks to the JIT Readers

Daniel Weigert
Kim Boyer
James Caplan
Kelly O'Donnell
John Ashmore
Michael Pendergrass
Peter Manis
Micky Cocker
Larry Omans
Paul Westman

If We've missed anyone, please let us know!

Editor
Lynne Stiegler

From Natalie

For M and T

From Michael

To Family, Friends and
Those Who Love
To Read.
May We All Enjoy Grace
To Live The Life We Are
Called.

BRAKALON

LUVENDI

UBUARA

———————

Tethra, one of the smaller cities on the planet High Tortuga, formerly known as "Devon," was a surprising amalgam of smells and commotion. Barnabas wove through the crowds, oblivious to the brightly-colored awnings and the street vendors' wares. He did not need to see the unique weave on the baskets or how a cook loaded spiced meat and vegetables into a pocket of bread.

He had seen plenty of cities in his day, and by this time he was no longer concerned with what they looked like. It was all about what they *felt* like. A planet's cities were the bellwethers of its success...or failure.

And Barnabas wanted to see High Tortuga thrive.

Why he had started *here* he was not sure. He could have gone to H'onu, the capital... such as it was. On a whim, however, he'd come here when he left the *Shinigami*. Tethra lay on another continent, one the AI had told him was marbled with ore deposits lying under a variety of terrain from gorgeous snow-capped mountains to jewel-like oases between the dunes of the northern deserts.

For some reason, however, the original inhabitants of Tethra had decided to build it squarely in the middle of what might charitably be called a marsh, or, more accurately, a swamp.

It was full of reeds and it stank, and Barnabas was fairly sure there was some alien version of mosquitoes flying around. They weren't as bad as mosquitoes on Earth—what *was*?—but they were no fun. Even with his reflexes, he had managed to hit himself once or twice trying to get one.

Whenever he did that he was fairly sure he heard Shinigami snickering in his head.

He spoke to her in his head as he walked so as not to attract the attention of the populace. *You know, in* my *day—*

Before humans figured out how to make fire, you mean?

Barnabas's face settled into a frown. He did *not* like rude people. Well, except *maybe* Tabitha, known to the inhabitants of High Tortuga and other former Empire citizens and enemies as "Ranger Two." Come to think of it, he wasn't even sure why he *did* put up with her.

In my *day*, he continued after a moment, *we raised the grain and herbs to brew our own beer and bake our own bread. We sewed our own clothes. We didn't rely on technology.*

Shinigami paused, which meant she was trying to calculate what he meant. He enjoyed the fact that she wasn't sure yet.

Is it your opinion that the inhabitants of this planet use too much technology, Grandpa?

Barnabas stopped and directed a glare skyward. *Did Tabitha stow away on the ship?*

No. Why do you ask?

It's the only thing that explains your attitude—that she's there egging you on. Barnabas linked his hands behind his back and strolled onward, passing a group who appeared to be primates of some sort. The spray of hair on their faces looked somewhat like that of a marmoset, but their coloring was a deep rich brown with a hint of dark red.

In addition to the pseudo-marmosets, he saw some beings who looked like slugs, and a tall, reedy looking species with green-tinted skin and black double-pupiled eyes that had no whites. They seemed to move along the edges of the streets, never wading into the crush.

So, why did *you mention the technology?* Shinigami asked.

Oh, now you're curious?

You left me floating up here. I'm bored.

There's only so much you could do down here.

There are a lot *of things I could do. I have guided missiles. I have a flamethrower. I'm exceptionally maneuverable, even in an atmosphere—*

You have a flamethrower?

There was a pause.

Shinigami! You have a flamethrower? Barnabas kept his mental voice quiet and calm.

He was very, very good at not losing his temper. He had in fact vowed never to lose his temper again. It was the only reason he allowed himself on-world anymore.

Maybe, the AI admitted. *I think Jean Dukes built it on a dare.*

Barnabas considered this. He was not sure whether he believed Shinigami, but—disturbingly—it did sound like the sort of thing the weapons people on the *Meredith Reynolds* would have done.

What do you mean, you think?

Well, I mean I heard them talking about installing something, and now I have a switch I could turn on to see what it does. In fact, let's try now.

No, no! Barnabas actually waved a hand in the air, earning himself some odd looks. *No. Let's not. We'll talk about this later.*

Why later?

Because right now, Barnabas told the AI with quiet satisfaction, *I'm going to go get a drink.*

He had seen a lot of cities in his day, and one thing never changed.

There was *always* somewhere to get a drink.

Venfaldri Gar settled down on a stool at the bar and tried not to frown too obviously.

Normally, he would not even think of coming to a place as grimy and rundown as this, but he needed information and a seedy bar was the surest place to get it.

He winced when the bartender came into sight. She was an Ubuara. The sprays of white hair on her cheeks marked her as a female, and his sensitive eyes could pick up a faint brindled pattern in her sleek coat.

The Ubuara were partially hive-minded; each had their own thoughts, and yet absorbed some of their group's thoughts in a very particular way. They could pass information to one another without speaking, and not simply words but also emotions and images. They had been observed absorbing each other's thoughts and making those thoughts their own, although they had also been known to act individually.

Only the Ubuara seemed to understand when either thing—group integration or independent action—might happen. There was an Ubuara language, half hand signals and half words, but it was rarely used—at least not out loud. They tended to speak to each other mentally and learn the local language wherever they ended up in their travels.

Gar did not like Ubuara. No business owner in their right mind did, especially not an overseer of Devon's mining industry. You could cut off their connection to the rest with a simple implant that transmitted a blocking signal—and of course, the cost of the implant was added to the worker's contract, to be paid off with a few extra months of work.

But maintaining the transmitters was simply One More Thing To Do... and the Ubuara tended to overreact when they were cut off from the rest of the group.

It was just for a year. You would think they would understand.

It was a business owner's nightmare, and Gar had long been of the opinion that Ubuara weren't worth the trouble. He wasn't in charge of staffing, though, and given that they tended to start insurrections if you *didn't* cut them off from one another, they had to be dealt with somehow.

The Ubuara swung over to him using a series of holds on the ceiling and tilted her head toward him.

"May I get you a drink, sir?"

"Fruit juice, whatever you have." Gar hesitated only a moment before adding, "Please."

"At once, sir."

She swung away, seeming pleased by the order. He had chosen it with care. The Ubuara enjoyed fruit juice, and he wanted her to think well of him. He *didn't* want every free Ubuara on the street to know who he was and keep him from getting the information he needed.

Namely, what was that damned ship that had just appeared in orbit? The last time a strange ship had appeared, the mines had been shut down the next day.

Or at least *most* of them had.

Gar hunkered down to try to make himself appear as short and wide as he could. For a Luvendi he was noteworthy. Tall and pale, his eyes had double pupils that were ringed with bright blue-green. Although unusual simply because of his appearance, he was also distinctive because so many of the mine overseers had been Luvendi.

That was why he was afraid the bartender might not like him. There was really only one way people got to this planet, and Gar was not foolish enough to believe that people *enjoyed* working in the mines.

He wasn't cruel, of course. He was only the vice-overseer, an assistant of sorts to Venfirdri Lan, who had once run many mines on Devon. Lan *was* cruel, and Gar always did his best to intervene when Lan's actions might result in an uprising.

A medium-sized bipedal alien entered as Gar was given his fruit juice, and Gar looked at it curiously. He hadn't seen this species before. It had a pinkish cast to its skin, eyes with a ring of color around the single pupil, and hands with no claws.

Gar gave it a once-over and pitied whatever overseer

had drawn the short straw and gotten this one as a worker. It didn't look very strong. Not interesting at all.

He scanned the bar and settled his attention on a group of Nekubi in the corner, their thick tails drawn under them to form makeshift seats. What were they talking about? Did *they* know about the strange ship?

Venfaldri Gar, of all people.

Aebura swung away from him with relief. He didn't seem to have recognized her, which was probably a good thing. Gar had never been as cruel as Lan, but she wasn't foolish enough to believe that Gar actually cared about the workers in their mine.

She had ended her contract two years ago and come to Tethra to wait for the friends she had made in the mines, starting her business in the interim.

She had believed that they would be along within a few months, so she'd held out on hiring help at first. She worked herself ragged to serve everyone herself, make the fruit juices, stock the back room, and clean the place.

But the months passed and no one had come.

She began to hear stories from the people who had left other mines, although they used the word "escaped." They told her that sometimes the overseers didn't like to let people go. Sometimes they added months to a contract for things like medical care to make it seem legitimate, but most of the time they didn't even pretend.

She had been angry. She had spoken with the other Ubuara in the city, learning their stories and about the mines they had worked in. She had found out that although Lan was the cruelest person she'd ever met, he wasn't bad as far as overseers went.

Then word had come recently that the mining corporation had been bought out and everyone was being freed. The contracts were terminated. The mines were closed down and would be reopened as legitimate businesses, with the workers receiving wages.

And *still* her friends had not arrived. Not a single one of them, over the years, had come to find her.

Aebura had kept collecting information, and she had noticed something very interesting—not one person she had spoken to had come out of Venfirdri Lan's mine.

It was possible she had just missed them. She knew that.

But she did not think so.

And so now she struggled with the idea of speaking to Gar about it. He would surely know the answer, but old habits died hard—like the one about not annoying the overseers. If he hadn't remembered her, her instincts told her she should keep it that way.

She swung over to a new patron. Lost in her thoughts, she hadn't seen this one enter. She had seen one or two aliens like this before, just a glimpse on the street, and she understood enough about the species to know this one was male. Oemuga, an Ubuara who had traveled to H'onu, said there were many humans there now. Aebura was curious to find out more about them. She supposed not many had a reason to come to a place as small and out of the way as Tethra.

"What can I get for you?"

He hesitated, then spoke with a slight accent. "What would you suggest?"

"I have fruit juice," Aebura offered. "All kinds."

His nose twitched slightly and the corners of his mouth moved, but she did not know what that meant in this species. He seemed to consider for a moment.

"Whatever kind you recommend," he told her finally. "Unless you have beer?"

"Beer?" She did not know that word.

He gave a very faint sigh. "I did not expect it. Fruit juice, then."

When she returned, the glass held steady by her back feet while she swung over to him, he looked up at her pleasantly.

"What's your name?"

"Aebura." She smiled. It wasn't unusual for patrons to want to talk, but usually they did that after weeks of coming in. "Who are you?"

"My name is Barnabas." His voice was nice, she decided. It was very smooth; easy on the ears. "I am new here. Tell me about this place."

"It is a very different place than it was a few months ago," Aebura told him. She found a rag and began to wipe glasses dry, still hanging by one arm as she did so. "The mines were all closed down. Most of them, anyway."

She hardly noticed it at the time, but her eyes drifted to Venfaldri Gar.

The alien noticed, though. He leaned forward, his eyes intent, and uttered only two words.

"Tell me."

2

The strange thing, Aebura thought later, was that she had told him everything without hesitation. There was something about him. He wasn't as tall as the Luvendi, nor did he have claws or sharp teeth or the sheer brute strength of the Brakalons.

But he had a commanding presence. When he spoke, you *wanted* to do what he told you.

So she told him the whole story, from her first days on Devon to the work in the mines to Lan and Gar and the rest of them. She explained how she'd been one of the first employed in Sector XVIII's Mine 2b—and therefore one of the first to leave—and how she had nearly forgotten the touch of the group mind by the time she was released.

She told him how she had waited and waited.

To her surprise, instead of offering her a platitude he considered her story in silence for a long time.

"Tell me about your contract," he suggested finally.

"You want to see it? I have a copy." She'd kept it secreted

away the whole time she was on the transport and in the mines.

Only now did she realize that she must have known on some level what kind of people they would be working for. Why would she have kept the contract unless she knew they would try to weasel and cheat their way out of it?

"Yes, please," the human requested politely. "I would love to see it. And if it's not too much trouble, I'd like another glass of this fruit juice. It's excellent."

Aebura glowed with pride since she made the fruit juice herself. "I'll go get it," she said and hurried away.

She didn't know it, but a fierce argument had started within the first minute of her telling her story—and it showed no signs of slowing down.

Why not? Shinigami demanded now. *It's a perfectly good solution. Why not do it?*

Because I am not a madman who burns down cities and then asks questions, Barnabas told her. His voice was terse. *That would be rank vigilantism.*

What's wrong with vigilantism?

It doesn't follow the rule of law. It isn't impartial.

What's not impartial about suggesting that slavery is wrong?

That isn't— Barnabas sighed and looked down at his empty glass of fruit juice. To his surprise, he really *was* enjoying the stuff. It wasn't beer, of course, but he couldn't hold that against it. Not everything could be beer. *Justice should be impartial.*

I don't see why.

You're being very difficult.

The Queen Bitch doesn't leave justice up to other people when she sees something bad going on. And you were a Queen's Ranger.

That was different. I was acting on her orders and enforcing her Justice.

There's only one Justice, and it isn't the same thing as laws.

When did you become a philosopher?

When did you become a coward?

Barnabas went still as stone and Shinigami, sensing she might have pushed things a little too far, withdrew into silence.

Aebura swung out of the back room and offered him a folded piece of paper. She noted curiously that Barnabas looked far angrier than he had when she'd left. She filled his glass with fruit juice, worried that he might be angry at *her.*

She'd only known him for a few minutes, but she instinctively knew she did not *ever* want to see him angry. She withdrew a little and busied herself with work.

Barnabas stared at the piece of paper and read. There was a low throb of anger in his gut.

Coward?

Cowardice had nothing to do with this. He had *wanted* to go off on his own. He would say that he was here because he knew there was still injustice to be rooted out. From what he had seen of the universe, there would *always* be injustice. There were always people who wanted to see what they could get away with.

He remembered how he had once been. He had completely lost control—everything that made him...well, not *human* perhaps, but sentient. He had cared for nothing more than what *he* wanted to do. He'd been ruled by his emotions, and other people had suffered for it.

He had sworn that he would never give in to that again. He had been comforted by the strictures of a monk's life and learned to strive for a higher standard of morality, and when he had joined Bethany Anne he had been glad to know that he served someone whose laws were truly just.

Someone who could take him down if he ever got out of control. She'd made that *abundantly* clear. Despite his mood, he smiled slightly at the memory.

Now he was out on his own because he needed to be. It was time for him to stop relying on anyone else to check him before he went too far.

He wasn't arguing with Shinigami because he *didn't* want to burn this whole place down, but because he *did*. He understood all too well why she had suggested it. He had wanted the same thing when he'd heard Aebura's story.

But he knew he needed to let go of the anger before he acted or he might do something he would regret. There was no one else to talk his plans over with now. There was only him.

Well, and Shinigami.

He shook his head wearily and closed his eyes and let the anger sink back into the recesses of his mind. That was the trick to this: you could always get rid of anger if you *wanted* to. Often he did not want to. Anger slipped into his mind with a comforting familiarity. It whispered for him to break the rules because he worked for a greater good.

And then when you weren't looking, you crossed lines and found yourself with more blood on your hands than you could ever atone for.

He was aware of the tall thin alien watching him as he beckoned the bartender over again. He gestured to the paper. "This is a standard contract, I'm afraid."

"I know." Her tail drooped sadly. "I didn't think I could get a better one."

"Mmm. Hear me out. It's standard, but it's utterly wrong." Barnabas pointed to a few paragraphs. "This basically indemnifies the mine owners for any danger they put you in and allows them to charge you for anything they want and add time to your contract. Here, it says that if you have a dispute about the contract you have a right to legal representation, but there are no provisions for how you're expected to go about obtaining that. In short, it's a mess."

She was quiet for a moment. "I wanted to leave, but no transports besides the mines' go from here to Dugan—my home planet. Even if there were, how would I have paid my passage? Dugan has no exports, really."

She was embarrassed, and she felt like an utter fool now. She had known that the contract was not in her favor. She had expected poor conditions in the mines, and she knew she would have to work hard, although she didn't object to that.

But she hadn't guessed that the mine owners wouldn't let people go at *all*. Because if you couldn't leave and you didn't get your wages until the end of your service year, how *would* you find legal representation?

What would stop people like Venfirdri Lan from doing whatever he wanted to the people he employed?

She should have known.

"Aebura." Barnabas sounded gentle. "People like this

prey on people who don't know better. You were caught up in something bigger than you."

Aebura hesitated, then dropped down from her perch to crouch on the counter in front of him. "It wasn't that," she explained. "I feel foolish, yes, but that was a small thing; unimportant. When I left the mines…"

She glanced at Gar again to see if he was watching and Barnabas felt a small stirring of anger.

She lowered her voice. "When I left the mines after my contract was done the others asked me to smuggle them out with me. They said that Lan was getting worse and they were afraid for themselves."

"You didn't do it," Barnabas guessed.

She shook her head. "I told them that they only had a few months more on their contracts. I told them…" Her small shoulders slumped. "It doesn't matter now. They were all excuses. I knew Lan was getting worse. We had less food to eat and the hours were longer. I told myself he wouldn't go this far."

"'This far?'" Barnabas echoed.

There was a pause while Aebura wrung her hands. She was rocking side to side a bit as well.

"Slavery," she blurted finally. "I think that when the mines shut down Lan didn't tell them, and he didn't let them leave. Why else would *none* of them come to Tethra? They never got out."

Barnabas nodded slightly toward Gar. "And that alien there—is he this 'Lan' you speak of?"

"Oh, no." Aebura smiled slightly. "That is Venfaldri Gar. He was Lan's second-in-command." A moment later she added, "I do not think he recognizes me. He never liked Ubuara. I think he thought we were all the same. Because of our minds."

Barnabas raised his eyebrows. "What about your minds?"

"We can speak telepathically," Aebura explained.

"Without implants?"

"Yes." Her tail twitched, which Barnabas thought might be a sign of amusement. "They need implants to *stop* us from doing it."

"Why would they want to stop you from doing it?"

Her tail was not twitching now. She hunched and would not meet his eyes. "They think we'll start a rebellion or pass prohibited materials if we're allowed to, so when you get your contract you get an implant that stops you from connecting. I don't know how it works."

Shinigami, scan the alien in front of me. I want to know about the implant in her head.

Shinigami was silent, and Barnabas wondered if she was still speaking to him.

A few moments later, however, she reported, *It is a device that transmits radio waves. It is placed near what are likely to be the speech and language centers of the brain.*

"Likely to be?"

I am guessing, based on physiology and what I can read of the brain waves, that this creature is very similar to a primate. The device would likely interfere with speech in more than one way, but it's difficult to know.

Thank you, Shinigami.

Barnabas considered this.

I still say we burn this sonofabitch down, Shinigami added. Apparently she had decided that it was once again time for her to express her opinions.

Barnabas's mouth twitched in something that might have been considered a smile. He remembered Michael saying that creating female vampires was riskier than creating male vampires. *Because they are more likely to fail?* Barnabas had asked. *No,* Michael replied, *because they talk. A lot.*

Shinigami?

What?

Why do we not like slavery?

There was a pause, and Barnabas knew that Shinigami —rightly—believed this to be a trap of some sort.

He waited.

Because it infringes on the rights of individuals.

Are you quoting something?

Shinigami did not deign to answer that.

Either way, Barnabas continued, *if you dislike slavery because it infringes on the rights of individuals, I can therefore assume that you would rather make people's lives better, not worse. If so, burning "this sonofabitch" down is illogical because...*

Silence.

I'm never going to let you use the flamethrower if you don't answer me.

Because burning to death would make their lives worse, Shinigami said sulkily.

Very good. Barnabas smiled at Aebura. "I apologize for that. I needed to have a conversation with my associate." He tapped his head. "We can also speak mind to mind in a way, but we require technology to assist us."

Which apparently you have some big objection to. What was your point about that, anyway?

That in my day tools like ships did not have minds. *They were simply inanimate objects, no more. They didn't talk back.*

How boring. And how error-prone, too. Have you met *any humans? They do stupid things. No wonder you gave us minds.*

Humans are not idiots. Barnabas resisted the urge to roll his eyes. They really should have given Shinigami to Tabitha. She'd broken Achronyx in, so surely she could have done the same here.

Name one thing a human can do better than me.

Strategize in unfamiliar situations?

No human will ever best me in strategy. Ever.

Wrong, Barnabas said flatly. *Strategy requires logic, emotion, and instinct. Though you may best us in logic simply by running simulations, you will never be an unqualified superior choice as a strategist.*

There was a very long silence—by Shinigami's standards, anyway.

Prove it, she demanded finally.

What?

Prove it. Play a game with me. Chess.

That's insane. The simulations alone—

I won't run simulations more than ten turns ahead. When he said nothing, she added persuasively, *On my honor.*

I'm still not sure artificial minds have *honor.*

Say that to Archangel II's face! I dare you.

I retract my comment. Barnabas narrowed his eyes slightly. *Very well, you have a deal.* He looked back at Aebura again with a smile.

All Aebura had seen was a brief moment of inattention.

Emotions had chased one another across his face and his lips had moved slightly, but she would never have guessed he was having a conversation.

How fast could he speak? How fast could he *think*?

She shivered slightly. This alien didn't look very threatening, but she was now firmly of the opinion that looks were deceiving on that front. Why, she wasn't sure. He hadn't done anything intimidating...yet.

She didn't know it, but that was going to change in approximately thirty seconds.

The alien to your left is trying to scan you, Shinigami reported.

Has he succeeded?

Impossible to tell. Your clothing is made to repel some scanners, but without knowing more about him and the technology he has access to I couldn't say.

Barnabas leaned forward slightly. "Aebura, what species is that man?"

"He's a Luvendi."

I could have told you that much, you know.

Not now, Shinigami. "What should I know about the Luvendi in general?"

"A lot of them run mines here. Their bones are fairly brittle." Aebura considered and concluded, "They don't have music."

"*Everyone* has music." Even if he despised most of it.

"Not them," Aebura argued. When she saw Barnabas's skeptical look she added, "Seriously!"

Barnabas looked at the alien and, having caught him staring, raised a single eyebrow.

Then Gar did something that seemed like a good idea at the time, but that he would later describe as the biggest mistake of his life.

He ran.

3

When Gar first took off, he didn't have any sort of plan at all. He just looked into the eyes of the small alien—pathetic looking, really—and felt a wave of inexplicably strong fear. It was a lone human.

But it was also affiliated with the former Etheric Empire.

He had learned that from the Nekubi in the bar, offering one a drink and looking away in disgust as it slimed its way up the barstool and sat. It had taken depressingly long to get it to open up at all. It was a clever bargainer, and Gar knew that with that example he was hardly going to get anything more out of the other two.

Besides, once he'd spent an agonizing half-hour buying it drinks, he was determined to have that time be worth something. Finally it opened up.

Strange ship in orbit? Oh, yes. Registered as the Shinigami, *yes, yes. Registered to the former Etheric Empire, yes. And I'm not saying I'm certain, oh, no, not certain, but the last time we saw aliens like that one over there was right before the mines got bought out. They're called "humans."*

At first Gar thought this was a joke. He had heard stories of humans. Their eyes glowed red, they had claws, and they could beat Yollins in single combat.

This was clearly not a human, but the Nekubi had been sure. It couldn't even identify whether the alien was male or female, but it was sure the thing was human. Absolutely sure.

And Gar began to wonder.

He still remembered the day things had changed. Well over two years ago, Lan had received an urgent message from the corporation they served. He had holed himself up in his office while he reviewed the message, then made sure all communications to the outside world were completely shut down.

Gar had assumed this was some sort of security protocol and accordingly, he waited to be briefed while he followed Lan's orders. He made sure there were no radios to be found anywhere on the premises, and no transmitters of any sort. He helped the security team take down the satellite uplinks.

Lan had never briefed him on anything.

What he *did* do, however, was enact all the rules he'd always said the mine *should* have. There were strict curfews now, and reading materials were confiscated. The workers were pleased to learn that they would now receive wages, but less pleased to learn that food would be available at a store and they now needed to pay rent for the little huts they lived in, the payments for which would be withdrawn from their wages.

When Gar told Lan about the increasingly dire mutters he was hearing Lan simply told him, "Do what you have to do."

Since then, Gar had done things he didn't like to think about.

It had started slowly; that was the thing. First, there were more people in the little jail, so he had to build a new one. The security guards complained too much, so he had the prisoners build it. They were surly and bad-tempered, so he had them whipped.

It was all very logical when he thought about it. The thing was, it left a sort of a sick feeling in his stomach.

And he was angry. He was angry all the time now. When he walked through the mining camp, it was with *his* eyes darting this way and that, to see which person would rebel next. And there was always another one. Why couldn't they just follow the rules?

It wasn't just them, either. Why couldn't Lan enforce some of his own policies for a change? He didn't have the workers yelling at him. *He* didn't see their stares. He just called for more and more supplies from the city and holed up in his office. He was snappish when Gar asked him to do anything at all.

Do what you have to do. Take care of it. Don't bother me with things like this.

Bastard.

Then yesterday, Lan had called him into the office. Gar was to go to Tethra. He needed to do something "of the utmost importance." When Gar found out that he was going to procure one of Lan's favorite types of cake, he didn't even care about the absurdity. He hadn't left the compound for months and he was beyond pleased to have time away from the sullen workers, the bored security guards—*there* was a recipe for trouble—and, above all else, away from Lan, who wasn't explaining why *any* of this had been necessary.

He didn't even care that he'd have to give a fake name and make sure he wasn't followed back. Nothing bothered him.

Until he'd started to piece together the whispers once he'd arrived in Tethra.

Until he realized that the mine Lan controlled should have been shut down entirely and the workers let out of their contracts—with pay, presumably, for the ones Lan had kept beyond their year.

Lan had told him that the company had a provision in the contracts for work shortages, and that workers would be paid double wages for staying past their year.

Gar was beginning to have the feeling that none of that had ever been true.

When he'd heard about the strange ship in the sky, and the other whispers that one like this had been seen months ago...well, he wanted to learn more. When he heard that the captain of that ship might be sitting in the bar next to him?

He ran.

If you had asked him later he would tell you that he hadn't known for a *fact* that there would be trouble. How could he have been sure, after all, that this ship and the other were connected to the mines shutting down? How could he have been sure that he would be held responsible?

But he remembered the things he had done and the sick feeling in his stomach grew, and he ran.

He ran out of the bar and into the little side street, shoving people out of his way. He was Luvendi; *they* should move out of *his* way so he wouldn't be hurt. But this place was a madhouse, made up of all former workers in the mines, and they showed the same appalling lack of order here they showed there.

"Move. *Move!*"

He ran until his breath gave out, which wasn't too long, really—embarrassing, but everyone got older—and then he bent over and waited for his hearts to stop pounding.

He was being ridiculous. This human had no idea who Gar was. How could he? Gar had given a fake name, and he had certainly not told anyone who he worked for.

Gar stood up with a sigh, turned around—

And saw the human staring at him from a few yards away.

Again, Gar would say what had happened wasn't so much a conscious decision as simple instinct. He pulled out his gun and fired, and he didn't even wait to see if the human was injured before he ran again.

He needed to get to one of the company houses. They'd been established by Luvendi who had decided to leave the mines and set up shop in the cities. One could hardly blame them, of course. Life in a city was far better than the life in a mine, even as a vice-overseer. The food was better, the lodging was better, and the company was certainly better.

Yes. One of those lodging houses would take him in, give him shelter. He knew of one on the outskirts that had always looked forbidding, with its heavy metal doors and few windows.

That one seemed best right about now.

He shot *at me*, Barnabas bitched. He was running, rather enjoying the feel of sunlight and fresh air on his skin. He didn't particularly mind living on ships, but he did miss the outdoors.

I could take him out. Shinigami's raspy voice held a note of anticipation.

With what, a guided missile? He ducked under a heavy basket being carried by two massive aliens. *Also, what were those?*

Maybe. And they're Brakalons.

Interesting. Barnabas caught sight of the Luvendi's pale head disappearing down an alley on the other side of the street and rerouted himself with a curse. Those long legs were damnably fast.

I'm assuming from your silence that you do want missiles. They'll be armed in ten seconds.

What? No! No missiles! He hurdled a fruit stand. *And since I know you're about to ask why, tell me how you're planning to avoid harming civilians?*

Tell me *how you're planning to catch the alien? What, are you out for an evening constitutional? Stop strolling.*

I'm running!

Not very fast.

That's a matter of opinion. You *don't even* have *legs.* This alley was disgusting. There were frogs in it, for God's sake. And slime. Barnabas was going to find whoever had decided to build in this swamp and make them drink bad beer until they gave up the will to live.

All right, how about an objective measurement? You're not going as fast as he is. It's time to—

No. No, we're not doing the red eyes and claws thing. People here don't know much about humans, and I can catch him without that. Just figure out where he's going and give me a path!

You are the most boring person I know.

I'll keep that in mind.

Go left when you reach the main street and go straight until you see the cathedral.

There's a cathedral? The Jesuits have always traveled widely, but I'll be really impressed if they've managed to get—

Cathedral, temple—whatever you want to call it. It has a statue on top that looks like a four-year-old made it. Shinigami considered. *And I don't know why you don't want to go all red-eyes. It's a good thing. We want humans to settle here, and we don't want other people to mess with them.*

I am not talking about this right now!

Mmmhmm.

Ahead of them, Gar was running like his life depended on it—because for all he knew, it *did*. He hadn't actually seen whether the human survived, after all.

Actually, it might be good to check that.

He looked over his shoulder, and for a moment could see only the usual assortment of aliens. Big and broad-shouldered, with the telltale gaps in the crowd where Nekubi were probably slithering around.

He was still there. *The human was still there.*

Shit. Gar started running again. He had the agonizing thought that he wasn't even going to die because this strange little alien killed him, he was going to die when his hearts exploded.

They certainly felt like they were going to. Had he ever run this much in his life?

There was the house. Finally.

Gar loped as fast as he could go, trying to wring more energy from his tired body. He pushed several smaller aliens out of the way to get to the door and held up an identification chip embedded in his long necklace, and when it opened he crashed inside. He slammed it shut behind him and slid down it, heaving for breath.

After a moment, aware of how ridiculous he looked and also aware that if anyone asked he would have to say the strange little human-thing hadn't actually done anything threatening, he got up and made his way up the stairs to the room he had always stayed in while he had been here before. He would alert the caretakers later.

He was halfway down the hall when he heard a noise behind him and turned to introduce himself to what he assumed was another tenant.

Red eyes glowed in the darkness of the corridor.

Gar gave a high-pitched scream and fled, slamming the heavy iron door of his room behind him as soon as he reached it. He backed away, heaving for breath. The human had gotten in. They must have hacked the keypad, which was terrifying enough—how had they faked a Luvendi genetic code?—but this door had no electronic lock. This door was safe.

But as he had been several times already today, Gar was very, *very* wrong.

With a screech of metal, the heavy door was ripped off its hinges and flung across the room. Gar scrambled backward, still screaming, and ended up in a puddle on the floor as the human, now red-eyed, advanced on him.

When Gar was pressed against the back wall of the room, the human paused to look at him thoughtfully.

"You didn't pay your bar tab," it murmured.

Gar gaped at him. *This* was why he'd been chased through the marketplace? This was why he was being confronted by a creature out of a nightmare?

"I...what?"

The human smiled, showing teeth that were definitely pointier than they had been at the start of this.

"Just kidding. Sit down. We're going to have a chat."

4

Barnabas had noted the way this alien had looked at him when he had come into the bar. The look had been brief and dismissive.

He understood why, of course. His skin was soft, or at least looked that way, his legs didn't have the characteristic structure that indicated quick acceleration, and he had no claws or sharp teeth. On the one hand, it made sense.

On the other, it had been a massive miscalculation on the Luvendi's part.

"What...what are you?" The alien was almost whimpering.

Get ahold of yourself.

Barnabas tried not to smile. *For once, Shinigami, I find I agree with you.* To Gar, he said, "I am a human. My name is Barnabas." He considered this. "You may call me Ranger for now."

Shinigami, we need to come up with a title.

I'll put it right at the top of our to-do list.

"Ranger" will serve well enough for now.

I was... I was joking.

The nickname seemed strange to Gar, but who could understand what humans called themselves or why? For a moment he half-remembered something—ranger, *ranger*… Where had he heard that before?

He wasn't going to put himself at a disadvantage by asking, but he'd had enough experience with this human already to think it was probably important. He'd have to see if he could get the human to tell him somehow.

Gar nodded courteously. "I am—"

"Venfaldri Gar," Barnabas interrupted. "Get up."

Gar stood up, trembling. His hands brushed the loose robes he wore to shield his normal clothes from the mess of travel through the swamp.

"Sit over there," Barnabas ordered. He pointed to a chair that had survived his assault on the room. Gar had to walk over the twisted wreckage of the door to sit down.

He arranged his robes carefully and placed his long-fingered hands flat in his lap, one over the other in a sign of respect. From such a pose, it was difficult to draw a weapon or strike quickly. Thus, it was a mark of respect. He wondered if the human knew that. Anxiously, he then wondered if the human might think it was an insult.

The human said nothing, however, only stared, with eyes that were fading from red back to brown. It stared, and it waited.

"Why are you here?" Gar asked it finally. He wanted to ask it how it knew his name, but that sounded like the sort of question someone would ask if they were afraid. He didn't want to *seem* afraid.

"That," the alien said with a smile, "is a very good question. A very good question indeed. A Ranger searches out corruption and injustice." He let the sentence hang in the air for a moment. "And cleanses it," he said finally, and almost pleasantly.

Gar knew almost nothing about humans, but even he knew the tone wasn't really pleasant at all. He tried not to swallow too obviously. Corruption and injustice, the human had said, and it *knew* who he was. Somehow it knew.

The human waited again.

I could use missiles.

I'm standing right here.

You would want to back up, then. I thought that was implied.

Infuriating. Barnabas prayed silently for patience and waited for Gar to speak. He didn't have *endless* patience, of course, but he had quite enough to wait for the Luvendi to figure out on his own that Barnabas was dangerous to him.

Finally, Gar spoke. "Why do you want to talk to me?"

Barnabas fought the urge to growl.

See, he's an idiot! You won't get anything out of him. Kill him with fire.

Not yet. Barnabas linked his hands behind his back and started to pace. "Why do you *think* I want to talk to you?"

"I don't have any idea," Gar replied. His face was—as far as Barnabas could tell—completely open.

Shinigami, tell me what you can about his stress levels.

If he's lying, you mean? He's definitely lying. You should—

Kill him with fire, yes, I know. There was an ominous pause and Barnabas hastened to add, *That was an acknowledgment that I'd heard you before, not something you should do.*

He then found out that when an AI grumbled it sounded a bit like an overworked computer.

He asked Gar, "Has anything that has happened in the past hour indicated that it would be wise to lie to me?" Gar said nothing, so Barnabas smiled again. He stopped pacing and looked directly at the alien.

And waited.

This time Gar wisely decided to try a different tack. "Maybe someone has told you that I am a..." His voice trailed off.

"Do go on."

Gar's mind raced. He could say he was vice-overseer at the mine, but this human might very well know that the mines should have been shut down. Would it count as injustice to him that they remained open and the workers weren't allowed to leave?

Yes.

So he couldn't admit that. But as the human—the *Ranger*—had pointed out, it wasn't wise to lie, either. This really was a mess.

"Perhaps I can make your choice easier," the human told him after a moment. Gar looked at him warily, and decided his wariness was clearly warranted when the human continued, "If you tell me the truth and I don't like what you say, we will have to have a conversation about how you intend to atone—and if you will be given the chance to. I acknowledge that this conversation might be unpleasant, but there may be a chance for redemption—and that's assuming I don't like what you say. For all we know, I might. If you *lie* to me..." he paused, "I'll rip your spine out."

Maybe, Gar reflected, that other human had bested King Yoll in single combat by terrifying it to death.

Maybe that had been *this* human.

"Do you have any other names?" he asked.

"A very strange question, given the topic at hand."

"I heard a story about one of your species who bested King Yoll."

"Ah. No, that was Bethany Anne." The human seemed to find this deeply amusing.

You should have lied.

That is entirely incorrect.

Ray, when someone asks if you're a god, you say yes.

What?

Watch a movie sometime.

Barnabas ignored that. "Now that we have established I am not the Empress, I suggest you answer my question. Why do you *think* I want to talk to you?"

Gar considered this. He was uncomfortably sure that when the human had mentioned ripping Gar's spine out, it had not been an idle threat.

"Because of my affiliation with the mines," he replied finally. He was very proud of his sentence, which did not suggest either past or present affiliation—until he saw the human's eyes flash.

Barnabas put one hand on either arm of the chair and gave Gar a very unpleasant smile. "Tell me about them."

"Dignitary..." he *really* wished he knew whether this one was male or female, "this is very aggressive behavior. By what authority are you questioning me? You will find yourself subject to both legal and trade penalties if you insist upon pursuing illegal interrogations."

"Oh, Gar." The human smiled again. "This isn't even *close* to an interrogation yet. You have no idea. And since you ask…"

He stepped back and spread his arms. Power crackled in the air around him and his eyes grew red once more. When he spoke, his voice carried the echo of many lifetimes and more deaths.

Gar shivered. Almost, he imagined himself back on Luvendan, watching the endless waves and listening to the hiss of the great beasts that circled their submerged homes. He had feared the Essekan all his life, and had fled Luvendan as soon as he had reached his majority.

This voice filled him with the same primal fear; that nothing he could do would protect him. There would be teeth and claws and the crushing black…

"My authority stems from a woman whom you should pray you never meet," Barnabas told him, "and *she* follows a higher law than any you have ever known. I was the first of her Rangers, and I mete out her Justice according to my conscience. If you were judged now, Gar, what punishment do you think you would deserve?"

Gar gripped the arms of the chair until his bones ached. His hands were trembling and he did not want to answer, yet he knew it would go badly for him if he did not.

"I think you would find me guilty of…slavery. I do not know your punishment for that."

Barnabas leaned close. "The punishment is death. The Empress has spread the word for many years that slavery would not be tolerated. Your mines were always close to the line, and what I heard in Tethra today tells me that the line has been crossed. Your words only confirm what I already knew."

Gar squeezed his eyes shut, but the image of the red-eyed human was seared into his mind. He could not escape it.

He would not plead; he would *not*. This human was like the Essekan, and not only in its raw power—*how* could it do these things?—but in the fact that Gar knew he could not bargain with it.

He's doing better than I thought he would. Possibly.

Agreed. He isn't pleading for leniency. I like that.

I'm confused as to why you've left him alive this long. Are you playing with your food?

I do not "play with my food" in any sense of the phrase, and he's alive because I need him to tell me where the mines are. The fact that no one has gone to storm the one Aebura mentioned tells me that they don't know where it is—and they probably don't know if there are more.

And you think this male will find out what you need to know?

He had better hope he can.

Shinigami snickered and Barnabas wondered briefly if her approval meant he was going in the right direction with this. At least she had stopped suggesting guided missiles or flamethrowers as the answer to this situation.

He turned his attention back to Gar. "Explain to me why you believe I would judge *you* guilty of slavery when, as I hear it, you are the second-in-command." His eyes flashed slightly. "But do not make the mistake of thinking I mean to excuse you."

"I would not." Gar's voice was surprisingly steady. He

took a deep breath and looked up. The panic was gone. He was still afraid, but he was calm now. "On the day the mines were freed—or should have been freed—our overseer closed us off from the outside world. I assumed that those were his orders from the corporation., but I was wrong about that. I learned today just how wrong."

Barnabas said nothing, just watched Gar carefully.

Gar straightened his back. If he was going to die, he decided, it would be with dignity. He had a dizzying memory of being back in the bar and thinking of the Ubuara with contempt. Thinking of this human with contempt. He could barely remember himself then.

He wasn't sure what had changed, but it was something very profound.

"However, I did things that I *knew* were wrong." He swallowed. "You speak of a higher law than the one I know, but the law I know is the company's law. Their rules. Even when I thought I was following those rules, I knew that some of the things I was doing were not right."

"Such as?" Barnabas's voice was silky.

"I… Well, I put down workers' revolts. They were angry that they hadn't been allowed to leave. I imprisoned many of them in our jail and increased penalties for infractions. Lan told me to take care of things, to make sure that everything was the way he wanted it, and I…"

He hung his head in shame. What could he say? He had become inventive…in the very worst ways.

"I did whatever I could to see his orders done," he finished quietly. "Even when I did not agree with them. Even when we were imprisoning people and they were only fighting to be allowed to leave—as we had promised them they could."

"I see. And what do *you* think your punishment should be?"

"You said the punishment was death."

He thinks death will be easier? Shinigami exclaimed. *A guided missile is too good for him.*

We agree again, Barnabas told her. He raised his voice. "I see from your eyes that you do not think death is a fitting punishment. I asked what *you* thought the punishment should be, not what *I* thought it should be."

Gar swallowed. All the memories were rushing back—whippings, long days in the cells, the workers growing thinner and thinner.

"Now you see," Barnabas told him softly. "You see that what you did cannot be made right. You see that death would be quicker and far less painful than suffering the same torments you devised for the workers. I expect you to think about that over the coming weeks."

Gar looked up at him in horror. What was the human planning to do?

"Tell me, do you know where all of the mines are on this planet?"

I could tell you.

An interesting point. But are you certain which were reopened under a legitimate business model and which were not? There was a pause. *I actually wanted to know.*

Oh. No, probably not.

We go with him, then. Barnabas waited for Gar to answer.

"No." The Luvendi shook his head. "I wish I did."

"If you were to go back, do you think you could find information on all the mines Lan oversees?"

"Most likely." Gar looked wary. "I've never been sure if he has others, but—"

He broke off as Barnabas leaned forward again.

"You will help me," Barnabas ordered, "and I suggest you pray that by the time you have finished helping me I believe you have redeemed yourself. You are lucky I need you, Venfaldri Gar. Otherwise you would already be dead."

5

"You mean to tell me you've never once played *chess*?" Shinigami sounded incredulous. Here on the ship she was able to project her voice, as well as a holographic image of herself seated in the chair across from Barnabas.

"Interestingly, no. I never got around to learning." Barnabas settled back in his chair and folded his hands over his stomach. "I have, however, read up on the subject. Ladies first."

Shinigami narrowed her eyes and a moment later one of the pawns slid forward. The game board displayed whatever game you wanted on its surface, and the pieces were holographs.

"Why are you staring at me?"

"You can project the *image* of a human," Barnabas observed, "but you do not *act* like a human."

"She often sat like this."

"And what did she do while she sat?" Barnabas queried. He moved one of his pawns—the one farthest to the right.

"I have no idea what you're talking about."

"You look like a statue." Barnabas focused on her pieces; she could slide her bishop into the space just vacated by her pawn. As he watched, she gave a silent command to the computer and made the move he had predicted. He looked back up at her. "You don't look at the board while you're thinking about your next move."

"I *am* looking at the board."

"You know what I mean. The holograph isn't doing the right things. You don't fidget. You don't pretend to move the pieces by yourself."

"Maybe accuracy isn't what I'm going for," the AI snapped.

"I think it is." Barnabas advanced the same pawn. "I think you'd like to be mistaken for a human when you want to be. It could be useful, after all. And it would allow you to play tricks on people."

"I *do* like that idea. What's your strategy with that pawn?"

"Why would I tell you?" While Barnabas watched her face, Shinigami caused the holograph's eyes to look at the board. "That's not bad. Bethany Anne would probably lean forward to look at it, though."

"Are her eyes bad?"

"There is nothing physically wrong with her. It's just a human mannerism. One tends to lean toward the thing one is examining."

"Humans expend energy in the oddest ways."

"Says the AI who suggested using a guided missile today."

"I still think that would have been a good strategy." She moved the adjoining pawn from her first one. "He's not going to help you, you know. I don't know why you brought him back."

Venfaldri Gar was presently sitting in the *Shinigami's* tiny brig. Barnabas would have preferred it if the brig had been made solely for humans, since everything would have been uncomfortably short for a detained Luvendi in that case. However, all Etheric Empire ships could accommodate a wide range of species, and therefore the ceilings were high and the benches were adjustable.

Barnabas had opted to bring the Luvendi back while he planned his strategy.

"I didn't want him to run away, and I might need to ask him questions while I formulate my plan."

"Make your next move. Even by human standards, you're slow."

"God help us if you ever meet a normal human being." Barnabas considered, then his mouth twitched and he moved his knight backward one space.

"What are you doing?"

"Playing chess."

"You can't move pawns backward!"

"Are you sure? Because I looked in the rulebook and it doesn't mention anything about that."

"*Why* would you move a piece backward right now?" The AI sounded pained.

"I don't expect you to understand my strategy just yet," Barnabas replied mildly. "I hope you'll catch on at some point, though. It would be very boring if I simply trampled all over you. One *does* hope for a worthy opponent."

The holograph flickered slightly, although the human

form was as still as a statue. Then she looked up and gave Barnabas a glare.

"Ah, you're learning. Good."

"I can't see how within the next ten moves you could hope to—"

"Then the only way you'll find out what I'm planning is to keep playing."

Shinigami stared at the board from all of the sensors that could see it. She had run ten million simulations so far, and the inescapable conclusion was that Barnabas had made an error in judgment or perhaps misunderstood the rules. Given the ways each type of piece could move, he was wasting valuable time and accomplishing nothing.

She moved a knight and waited to see what he would do.

Infuriatingly, he moved the pawn back to where it had just been.

"What are you *doing*?"

"Keep playing," he told her inscrutably.

"Fine. And what *is* your plan?"

"Do you actually want to hear it in order to be informed, or do you want to hear it in order to tell me it's foolish?"

"Probably both, if I'm honest."

"You've *definitely* been spending too much time with Tabitha. Very well." He moved the pawn on the far side of the board. "I am going to approach Venfirdri Lan as a missionary and tell him that I will be able to restore order to his mine. Once I have been able to assess what other mines he might be running, as well as learn more about his connections and the way the mine operates, I will make sure the workers are allowed to leave and that those in charge of keeping them there are held responsible."

"You just managed to make *freeing slaves* sound boring. This is a jailbreak! Have some fun with it!"

Barnabas frowned. "Who programmed you?"

"You know that's not how AIs work."

"Well, however it happened, you've acquired a very disturbing sense of humor along the way."

"I know." Shinigami grinned, flashing her razor-sharp teeth She did not sound very disturbed. "But your plan is really terrible."

"Why?"

Shinigami echoed his earlier words, "Do you actually want to hear it in order to be informed, or do you want to hear it in order to tell me it's foolish?"

Barnabas sighed. "To be informed."

"Boring again." Shinigami, he noticed, was making very cautious moves. She moved another pawn now. Almost her whole line was forward, though he noted that she kept the channels open for her bishops. "But since you ask, what do you really need to *know* about this? You could go in there and kill all the guards without breaking a sweat—"

"You don't know that."

"I do. I found four enclaves in the surrounding area that might be the mine we're looking for. None of them have security you couldn't handle on your own."

"I retract my criticism then."

"I like it when humans admit they're wrong."

Barnabas raised an eyebrow. "You know I'm not fully human."

"Close enough in this case. Your move." She sank into silence as he considered his options.

He really was very stubborn. She'd spoken about that with other AIs, none of whom seemed to have big opinions about Barnabas. *He's very quiet,* ADAM had said. He'd thought for a long time after that—long enough that Shinigami wondered if he'd short-circuited, but eventually he'd said, *I like him.*

TOM had agreed later. *He's very quiet. And very old-fashioned.*

But?

But Tabitha respects him. And he did win that beer-brewing contest very sneakily.

Very *sneakily,* ADAM agreed. *They still don't know about that.*

Shinigami, upon learning the details of the contest, had decided that she might like working with Barnabas. He was making it very difficult, though, being all prickly and honorable.

"Are you worried about having to kill them?" she asked finally.

"What?" Barnabas frowned up at her as he made an embarrassingly bad move. He was now blocking his rook with his knight, and his bishops were locked in place.

If Shinigami'd had a physical head she would have beaten it on the game board in frustration. She had been confident that she would win this strategy challenge, but she had expected it to at least be interesting. Barnabas was, however, making her wonder if she'd overestimated him.

She made another move. "It seems like the sort of thing humans have qualms over. Killing."

"Have you ever *met* any of Bethany Anne's people? Aren't you—"

"I am, and yes, I have. But I don't see why you, especially given all I've read, are trying to make this unnecessarily complicated."

"Everything is complicated," Barnabas replied absently. He moved another pawn. "In simple ways. It's one of my favorite paradoxes about the world. Although in this case, well…"

"What were you going to say?"

"Say I go in there guns blazing and get to the overseer, and I take all the information I want directly out of his head. The slaves are instantly freed and the slavers pay for their mistakes. Everything is tied up very neatly, yes?"

"Yeeesssss," Shinigami drawled cautiously.

Barnabas gave a pointed look at one of the sensors.

"I may be limited in the number of simulations I can run on the chess match, but I can go through as many as I want for this mission and that's a very easy way to—"

"You only ran them on the *mission*, didn't you?" Barnabas raised his eyebrows.

"Well, yes."

"And what *we* want is to make High Tortuga safe for habitation by our people. We want to know everything that's happening. We want to know who might come looking for it. Yes, this is one mine with an overseer who deserves to be dead, but what questions have I not yet thought to ask that might hint at bigger issues?"

Shinigami was silent for a moment. "You always think like this? You were a Ranger."

"I'm not sure what you mean."

"A Ranger sees injustice and goes after it. I thought the job was quite limited in scope."

"*Nothing* is limited in scope." Barnabas moved his left knight into one of the spaces left empty by a pawn. "That is what I have learned over the years. Do you know why I serve Bethany Anne?"

"Explain."

"Because she doesn't let things like definitions and laws keep her from doing the right thing. She makes use of them when it's warranted and does the right thing when they would hinder her. I would never let a narrow definition of the word 'Ranger' preclude me from doing what I believe is the right thing to do. I wouldn't then and I certainly won't now, when I'm not even a Ranger anymore."

"I don't think I'll ever understand humans." Shinigami sighed. "But I like them."

"Thank you. I'm assuming that was a compliment."

"It was. Are you *sure* you have a plan for this game?"

"Yes."

"Your moves so far suggest that you don't."

"I have a plan," Barnabas assured her. "Both for the game and for the mine, although in the latter case it's more of a structured non-plan."

"Have you thought of going into politics?"

"First you say you like me, then you insult me."

Shinigami snickered. "I wasn't sure you'd notice."

"And we were getting along so well. In any case, I stand by it. This is as good a place as any to begin learning what I need to know about this planet, and I have a perfect setup now."

"That Luvendi is a coward."

"I wasn't speaking solely of him. I meant having a link both to the mines and to the cities. High Tortuga is shaped now by the fact that many of its citizens didn't *choose* to go there; they just wanted to get away from where they were. They got there via the mines, and now they're establishing the cities. But there's another level of society: the people who made money off of the workers. If I cultivate knowledge of the mines and the cities, I can gain a perspective on the whole."

Shinigami wondered about that. She had run simulations and researched similar places, and she did not think highly of Barnabas's chances to do anything *other* than bomb the mines to smithereens.

After getting the civilians out, of course.

Mostly she wanted to try out the flamethrower.

"What do you think, Shinigami?" Barnabas asked. He made another move, apparently not seeing that he was far too late to accomplish anything in this game.

"I think that the two groups aren't as separate as you think," Shinigami told him. "In systems where one group controls power and wealth, the other group is rarely cohesive in its approach. You should expect spies. You should expect people to defend the ones they serve."

"That's a very interesting point." Barnabas was pleased.

"One other thing."

"Yes?"

"Checkmate." Her voice was smug.

"Well, look at that. I believe you're right." Barnabas smiled. "And so you fell for my first trap."

"It's checkmate. There's no way for you to win."

"I wasn't trying to."

"You were playing for a purpose *other* than to win?"

"Exactly." Barnabas switched off the game board and smiled up at one of Shinigami's sensors. "Lesson One about strategy: make sure you know what your opponent's goal is."

He left Shinigami sitting in incredulous silence and made his way to the brig to explain matters to Gar.

6

G ar could not figure out for the life of him what had happened.

Yesterday he'd been feeling entirely normal. He had done his job. He'd had all his old frustrations and all his old goals. He had enjoyed his foray into the city, of course, but he'd been prepared to go back to work without complaint.

Then a terrifying alien had chased him through the streets of Tethra, interrogated him, and even threatened to kill him...and somehow all Gar could think about was that he was deeply, deeply ashamed of himself.

It didn't make any sense. It had been so brief a time since everything had been normal.

Or was that correct?

He had been pacing around the ship's tiny cell, but now he paused. No, now that he thought of it, things had *not* been normal. If they had been *normal*, he would not have admitted what he had done as if it were a crime. There had been fear, yes, but hardly anything approximating torture.

The alien had asked him a few questions and the truth had spilled out.

For the first time in many years, Gar let himself wonder what his grandfather would have thought of who he'd become. The male had always been supportive of Gar's studies and his efforts to get off Luvendan.

He had died several years before Gar reached his majority, which had simplified things. Without him there, Gar never went back to visit. There was no one there he cared to see, and he imagined they felt the same way.

Ambition was frowned upon on Luvendan. The ambitious few left, giving aliens a rather skewed perception of the Luvendi as a whole. The Luvendi out and about in the universe did not answer to their government and had no desire to go back or enrich their planet.

For years that had been enough. Gar had looked no farther than the next promotion or the best way to spin an event to his advantage on a resume.

Now he wondered how many things like this he had done. He had laughed with the others when he'd heard workers complain about the conditions on the transport ships. *Had they thought they would get fine hotels and personal chefs?* He had been impatient even when his colleagues had complained about the company's archaic rules. They should have learned those rules and used them to their advantage.

Even his grandfather, who had supported Gar's ambition when no one else did, would not have been proud of the person Gar was now. He was uncomfortably sure of that.

He looked up as the door opened and the alien stepped into the room. Again, Gar was struck by how fragile this human appeared. Perhaps that was why they triumphed so often.

No one knew to be afraid of them.

He did not know it, but Barnabas was having similar thoughts. Aliens with such brittle bones that they apparently did not walk on crowded streets should surely not have risen to prominence, should they? Barnabas thought not.

The universe was endlessly confounding.

To Gar's surprise, the Ranger's first question was, "Is it true that your people do not make music?"

"It is true." Gar inclined his head. "Although some develop a taste for it." He lifted one shoulder as if to say he did not understand that at all. "It seems always to be a surprise when other aliens learn of it. Humans make music then, I take it?"

"We do," Barnabas confirmed.

"Why? I have never been clear on the purpose of it. Surely there are more productive ways to spend time."

Barnabas considered the matter, which surprised Gar. He expected the human to be far more brusque and tell him it was none of his business or not important. Instead, he seemed to be deciding how best to explain the matter.

"Do you tell stories?" he asked finally. "Fictional stories? Legends, perhaps?"

"Yes." Though Gar had hated those. They were repetitive, with the poorly-disguised moral that one should stay at home on Luvendan.

Barnabas looked intently at the expression on Gar's face. "Did you never have emotions so strong you could not find words to describe them?" he asked curiously. "Did you never encounter a truth so profound that it could not be told directly? Music, like stories, helps us say things we could not say any other way."

Gar considered this...and came to the inescapable conclusion that all other aliens were quite mad. "You mean to say that this *music* tells you stories?"

"Not precisely, although sometimes it does. It evokes strong emotions. It helps us praise God."

Gar blinked.

The alien mimicked his shrug. "If it is of no use to you, then it isn't. I was merely curious. In the meantime, we should discuss your return to the mine."

Gar felt a jolt of panic.

"I will need you to return," Barnabas told him, "and do a few things for me. For one, you will take this communications unit and provide me with information when I require it. We will determine a time of day for regular communications."

He handed the unit to Gar and indicated that the Luvendi should come into the ship with him. They went back the way they had come in, presumably toward the very strange shuttlecraft with no visible propulsion.

"In addition," Barnabas said, "when I arrive you will help convince Lan to admit me to the grounds."

"What should I say?"

"You know him best. Say whatever will convince him." Barnabas led the way into the shuttle bay and gestured to one of the black Pods. "Additionally, you will make yourself aware of security patterns. Guard rotations, who is sloppy and who is methodical, where the best and worst places would be to defend the mines. Anything you do not know already you will make yourself aware of. I will at some point want to hear a report on the strengths and weaknesses of the mine's security."

Gar stepped into the Pod, considering.

"And if I don't cooperate?" That was not his intent, but he wanted to know what would happen if the human believed Gar had failed him.

He was immediately sorry he had asked.

Barnabas's face clouded over. "Then I will do what must be done without your help."

The words were mild, but the intent was clear.

Gar shuddered as the door closed and he was alone in a Pod hurtling toward the planet below.

Aebura had just finished polishing several glasses when the human walked into her bar once again.

She said nothing, but settled down on the bar and wrapped her tail tight around her feet. She was not sure how she felt about him being back. The last time he'd come he'd chased Gar away, and such a disturbance might affect her bar. It might even ripple back to the mine somehow.

Besides, she had been working up her courage to speak to him. She had come to the decision that she could not wait any longer. She had to take action to find the mine—no one knew precisely *where* the mines were—and free people.

She didn't have a plan yet, but she knew what had to be done.

"Hello, Aebura," the human began courteously. "Do you have time to speak with me about the mines you mentioned?"

Aebura considered this, and let her fur fluff up and then smooth out. She was gratified that he had remembered her name and willing to hear him out.

To her surprise, the human seemed to understand the gesture. He took a seat at the bar and asked, "Should I keep my voice low?"

"As a precaution, yes." Aebura was curious. "What happened with Venfaldri Gar?"

The human smiled, and it did not look like a particularly *kind* smile. "He went back to the mines, but he now works for *me*."

That's an optimistic assessment of the situation.

Not now, Shinigami.

Aebura's tail lashed. "Why would you trust him?"

You see? Shinigami asked. *She understands.*

What did I just say?

To Aebura Barnabas replied, "Because I have asked for his help in a very limited capacity, and he knows that his only chance of mercy lies in fulfilling my requests. More accurately…" He sighed. "Never mind."

"I would like to know," Aebura assured him.

"Very well. I want his help, but it is not *that* which will give him a chance at mercy. What I must see from him is an understanding of the wrong he has done, and the will and effort to set it right—and never do such things again. Will he do it?" Barnabas shrugged elegantly. "I don't know.

However, I trust him to do the things I asked him to do for me."

"What *did* you ask him to do?"

Barnabas explained the plan quickly. It was only a brief overview, but it covered the points that would be relevant to her. At the end Barnabas asked, "Is there anything you think I should know before I visit the mine?"

Aebura did not hesitate. "You should take me with you."

"Are you sure that's wise?"

"Yes. They can't tell us apart anyway. And we're useful. We can climb things and steal things, get into places where they don't think we'll fit."

Barnabas smiled. "Perhaps I will call on you to come to the mine, then. But not yet, I think. You are safe from the mine now, and you told me that this business was meant to employ and house your fellow workers. Do not jeopardize that yet."

"What use is it if they do not escape?"

"Aebura, I promise you this: if I need your help in order to free them I will ask for it. For now, I am not asking because I believe I can free them without putting you in danger."

Aebura considered the human's words and wavered slightly. She wanted to do this herself. She knew Gar underestimated her, and therefore she might have a small advantage.

But this human had been able to make Gar turn to *his* side, something Aebura would never have considered possible. She had to ask herself if he *underestimated* her or just had no reason to fear her. That made her feel very small.

Barnabas guessed what she was thinking. "In a perfect world, Aebura, you and I would not have met this way. But we don't live in a perfect world, and so I use my talents to stop injustice. There is no shame in not being like me. I have, shall we say, *talents* that make me well-suited to this job."

And a ship with guided missiles. Let's not forget that.

Let's not spread it around everywhere, either. You know what's better than taking someone out with missiles?

Nothing.

Wrong. Taking someone out with missiles they didn't even know you had.

I could accept that as a theory. The looks of surprise must be priceless.

Shinigami. If you use missiles, you don't want to be standing close enough to see the looks on their faces.

Aebura scratched contemplatively at the puffs of fur on her cheeks as a thought occurred to her. "If you disabled the radio device the Ubuara would be able to communicate with one another again. Lan doesn't like to do work, so he never goes out to check the equipment. It's either Gar or the security teams that keep an eye on it."

"That's good to know, thank you. Having people who can communicate silently about security guards and so on would be very useful."

"Oh, yes!" Aebura bared her teeth in what Barnabas assumed was an Ubuara smile. "That's why they don't want us to be able to do it. Also, you should talk to Leiguba."

"Who is he or she?"

"*He* is another Ubuara, and someone who was always very angry about the injustices." Her tail lashed angrily. "If you see him… If you see him, tell him I have not forgotten him, and that I will help him. I have no right to say it, having left him there for so long, but... I am doing what I can to make it better now."

"I will tell him," Barnabas promised.

———

The past few nights had been chilly, and Leiguba curled gratefully into the huddle of Ubuara in one of the huts, using their body heat to help keep himself warm. His body, aching after a day of working in the mines, began to relax slightly.

Even this felt hollow, however. If this were home or anywhere else that Ubuara could live as they were meant to he would be surrounded by emotion and the warmth of thoughts, not just bodies.

At home, he would have heard his younger sister murmuring to herself sleepily as she drifted off. Her thoughts at night were always cozy—what she'd had for dinner, the way her feet were tucked tightly against her to stay warm. His father liked to plan for the next day, and he was logical and precise. His mother drifted to sleep so quickly that all Leiguba felt from her were little moments of emotion from her dreams. His sister told him that his thoughts felt like wind through the trees on a summer night, a contemplative search through the day's memories like a breeze rustling leaves.

He should have known these Ubuara that way, but he hadn't had the chance. Their minds had been made mute on arrival and they existed in an unnatural silence.

A silence he knew he could not expect to end. A silence that might persist until he died here.

The thought panicked him and he opened his eyes, staring at the glint of moonlight through the holes in the wall. He couldn't live like this anymore. He couldn't.

He had to escape.

7

Gar had left three days ago and he still wasn't back. Venfirdri Lan drummed his long fingers on the desk and tried to control his frustration.

He couldn't help the sneaking suspicion that Gar had left for so long to make a point. Recently he had, quite frankly, been a pain in the ass. He had complained about duties. He had questioned orders.

He was also dangerously close to figuring out that Lan had no legal right to be running this mine. Lan hoped Gar would have the revelation soon, thus getting it out of the way—and at the same time, he also hoped that Gar would never figure it out.

The male was unpredictable, after all—a very strange mix of pragmatic and moralistic. Who could say what he might do when he learned the truth?

Lan really should start bringing a guard with him.

Or not. The guards didn't know either. Lan had fed them a story about their contracts being renewed and him fighting it, and he could hardly afford for one of them to overhear the truth at this juncture.

No, if things went wrong, he'd take care of Gar himself.

In the meantime, he *was* fairly certain that Gar was trying to make a point about how indispensable he was—or at least how much he ought to be compensated for his work. He knew it would be difficult for the overseer to find someone to take his place, especially with all the new duties.

So he was staying away, which forced Lan to do all the tasks Gar would have usually taken care of...and it was *exhausting*. The security guards were always complaining about *something*, the workers had formed groups that they were very carefully *not* calling unions, and the jail cells were so overfilled that the guards were concerned about riots.

As if that weren't enough, there were several technical systems in dire need of repair. Normally it would have been a small mountain of paperwork to submit claims to the company—unpleasant but doable—but now Lan was left wondering just how they were going to find a technician to come out here and fix things...and not mention the location of the mine to anyone after he left.

He knew he was on borrowed time. It would only be so long before the company's new leadership decided to make absolutely sure all the mines had been closed or the land was sold out from under him.

But he'd taken the gamble that he'd be able to pull it off for long enough to retire by disappearing quietly with a hefty sum of money.

That was if everything went right—and really, he

should begin thinking of buying Gar's silence. Lan tried to comfort himself with the thought that Gar really *had* been very pragmatic in his actions. It was just the occasional sentiment here or there that had been off, not a sudden onset of morality.

That would have been troubling.

Yes, Gar had made a shrewd move by staying away so long, and Lan could appreciate that. He would raise the male's pay and make it subtly clear that, in return for Gar's silence, he would have a share of the profits and assistance in getting away when people finally found them. It was tricky doing things like this—the underlings tended to get greedy—but Lan could deal with that when the time came.

With that decided, he was surprised to hear a door open nearby and the sound of Gar's voice. He looked up as Gar came into the room with a package.

The vice-overseer bowed respectfully. "My very deep apologies, Overseer Venfirdri. It was more difficult to acquire the goods than I anticipated, and I lingered in hopes of finding a technician to repair some of our systems —but I am afraid none could be found. I will return to my duties at once."

He laid the sweets on the desk and made to leave with another respectful bow, but Lan stopped him.

"Before you go?"

"Yes?"

Well, this was awkward. Lan wasn't quite sure how he wanted to approach it.

"What were you planning to do now?"

To his surprise, a secretive look flitted across Gar's face. "I was intending to, ah...inspect our security. I think that would be wise. The guards have been complaining. Yes. Faulty equipment."

He was almost babbling, and after a moment Lan came to the conclusion that Gar had *really* been planning to go and rest after his journey.

You can't expect a promotion unless you work hard, Gar. He decided to throw the other male off by accompanying him on his rounds as a little test of sorts. If Gar accepted his company with good grace, Lan would offer him the raise and promotion. If not, Lan would wait a little longer and think carefully about his next moves.

He stood. "It's a fine day. I'll walk with you."

Gar frowned for a moment. "It was beginning to rain."

"Still, I have been shut up in here all day. I will accompany you." Lan's voice brooked no argument.

"Of course." Gar acceded with a nod.

They strolled down the hill from the overseer's hut. It was nothing much to look at from the outside, though Lan had finally made it almost civilized inside. The rough board walls hid thick curtains that kept out the chill of the mountains, and rugs covered the floor. He had good lamps and a decent bed, as well his desk and chair.

Outside, however, the path was plain dust and the view was of the huts, walls, and grimy industrial-lit mine entrances.

Lan rarely came outside anymore.

At his side, Gar laced his hands behind his back in an attempt to appear nonchalant and thought furiously. It was unlike Lan to take any interest in running things—and why should he do so *today*, of all days?

Gar had planned to do his assessment of the security

systems before Barnabas had any time to think he was not upholding his end of the bargain. He feared that if Barnabas took care of things on his own, it might be a great deal more violent than Gar could survive.

And now Lan wanted to come along and...what, inspect the security measures? That couldn't be right. He must suspect something about Gar's trip, and Gar was worried.

"How was the city?" Lan asked.

"Very busy." It was hard to tell if this was a safe topic, and he tried to find a subtle way to set Lan's mind at ease. "The food is better, but there's never any company worth having."

Lan laughed. "No, there isn't. It's hardly a city, is it?"

Gar remembered the crush of color and sound. It had been overwhelming in a good way after the endless dust and grime of the mines. He knew the correct answer to the question, however. "A fitting city for a backwater."

"Anything notable?" Lan pressed as they reached the bottom of the slope and the doors swung up to let them through the walls.

The walls, of course, were not made to keep anything *out*.

Gar led the way up the stairs and onto the walls. He wondered if Lan would even realize this was an unusual sort of inspection. Lan knew so little about how this place was run.

"Nothing in particular," he replied, trying to sift through his head for safe topics.

If he mentioned a lot of people Lan might think he knew about the mines being freed, and Gar was afraid that if the overseer found out he knew, he might simply kill him and be done with it. But if Gar pretended not to know anything, against all odds, the other Luvendi might be suspicious.

Gar made his choice in a split-second and looked up and down the wall to ensure they were alone before stopping to look at Lan intently.

"We need to be cautious," he said quietly.

Lan raised an eyebrow. He was careful not to say anything that might be incriminating.

"There *were* technicians in Tethra," Gar lied, "but I couldn't trust any of them. I don't think anyone has noticed yet that our mines are still running, but word could get out so easily. How are we planning to keep this quiet?"

His words had been carefully calculated. He used "we" and he spoke without any distaste in his voice—he hoped. It was imperative that Lan think Gar was on his side.

For a moment Lan looked startled. "You knew." It was a question, despite the flat inflection.

"Certainly." He should have, anyway. "You never discussed it, but why else would you take our communications offline?" He really had wondered about that, so he gave Lan a piece of the truth. "I had actually thought that you were breaking away from the company."

"You didn't object?" Lan's eyes narrowed slightly.

"What does the company truly know about running a mine?" Gar asked fiercely and without hesitation. He knew all the correct things to say, even though they sickened him. "They like to talk about rules, but they don't understand how it is. They don't seem to care that if we followed every rule we would be bankrupt."

Lan looked wary but pleased. "And now that you know the truth?"

Gar waved a hand dismissively and tried to say what he thought Lan would say in his place. "We're supposed to just close down a working mine? What good would *that* do anyone?" He considered going farther and saying that surely the company must owe them more than that, but he decided not to do so. Best not to look like a caricature.

"Good, good." Lan seemed to have come to a decision. "I am glad that you understand."

"Of course." Gar smiled. "Should we go on? I had wanted to inspect any potential weaknesses in the case of any trouble."

"I trust you to do so," Lan told him magnanimously. "I will return to my work for now."

What work? Gar thought contemptuously, but he said nothing.

"We are glad to have you back," Lan added, and he went back down the stairs and toward his hut.

He was considering his options. He had intended to give Gar more money to keep his mouth shut, but it seemed there was no longer any need to do that. And in business one should never spend money when one didn't have to do so, of course.

Anyway, the whole thing had been his idea. He deserved to reap all the rewards.

He didn't realize yet that those rewards might not be as positive as he was expecting.

Gar's hands were clenched behind his back as he watched Lan leave.

It was clear what Lan wanted: to have the mines continue working for his sole benefit. Lan was many things, but he was not stupid about business. After this conversation, Gar knew exactly what the overseer was planning: to get away with this as long as he could, cutting all possible corners to make the most profits for himself, and when the whole thing either collapsed or authorities came for him Lan would run away with the money.

This was all about Lan, and Lan's interests.

Gar knew he could stride up to the overseer's hut and demand that he be compensated fairly. He probably should have done so, in fact. Sooner or later Lan would realize that it was strange for Gar not to have bargained at all with the information he revealed.

Would he have done so if he had not met Barnabas? He was afraid he might have.

He began to walk along the walls slowly, taking great care to inspect the construction and the electrical panels he could see. Lan would tell the guards what Gar was doing, so he no longer needed to worry that people would find his behavior odd or suspicious.

But it was difficult to look down on the camps from here and think about what was going on below. He could not tune out the little details he saw now; the way the guards watched the miners, the miners walking with slumped shoulders, the huts' shoddy construction.

How had he allowed himself to be caught up in something like this? Had it happened in small increments or had he blinded himself to everything in his haste to get off Luvendan?

Those questions might be productive later, but they weren't useful now. Gar tuned his thoughts out.

He could see places where the guards would easily be able to control crowds or get at people trying to escape, but there were a few stretches of wall that weren't easily accessible to them. One of the guard towers had recently suffered an electrical failure and the guards weren't manning it anymore. There was also a place where people had been dumping waste from the mines. Not only would it be difficult for the guards to reach anyone trying to break through the wall there, they might not even notice.

Gar just wished he knew what Barnabas's plan was— and how soon he could expect the human to arrive.

8

The transport ship shuddered as it hit High Tortuga's atmosphere. Carter Eastbourne ran a hand through his thick brown hair and sighed. He wanted *off* this ship already. It had been days since he'd had fresh air in his lungs, and...

Well, he should be honest. The *Meredith Reynolds* had really spoiled him. The air purification systems there ran like a dream, the lighting didn't hurt his eyes, and the food was good. He could get anything he wanted there.

Contrast that with the alien transport ships—worn down and poorly maintained, with food that barely deserved the designation.

Which really left the question of what he was doing here.

The thing was, living in established settlements full of humans might be more comfortable in some ways, but it didn't scratch "that itch." Carter's wife, Elisa, used that term with weary affection.

It was a big part of what had led him to leave Earth

with Bethany Anne's group. It wasn't *just* that he'd spent years being frustrated by the total inability of governments on Earth to, well…govern. He'd known since he was a little boy that there had to be *more* than just life on Earth. There was more to explore. There were places to go and things to figure out.

In a way, he *wanted* to be traveling on ratty old ships and eating awful food. Those would make good stories for later, when he was growing old in a house he'd built with his own two hands and he had his family all around him.

And in the meantime? Well, he'd be seeing things no human had ever seen before and carving out his place in the universe.

When they'd been told about High Tortuga, he'd been one of the first to volunteer. He'd left Elisa with the twins, Alanna and Samuel, and come here to find them a new home.

But not in H'onu. No, Carter wanted to carve out his own little square of the world, somewhere less traveled. He wanted to be surrounded by the unfamiliar, building things from the ground up.

Elisa had asked him before he left if he had any ideas about how to make money when he settled in. When he'd said he didn't have one she'd given him a Look, the sort of Look that made you realize just how foolish you'd been to underestimate her.

The truth was, he *did* have a plan—but it was risky.

It was *very* risky. He knew he should be grateful to Bethany Anne for leading the way to the stars, and he really was. He didn't want to disagree with her on anything because he knew her morals were the absolute gold standard. He could never have left Earth or lived as long as he had without the technologies she and the Empire had made commonplace.

It was just, well...Carter liked Pepsi.

He knew for sure that if he were to set up a bottling plant on High Tortuga there would be plenty of business. There were others living in the shadows of the *Meredith Reynolds* who thought like he did. He'd even heard that Nathan Lowell was one of them. Carter knew the old saying: where there's risk, there's money.

Bethany Anne was only part of the risk, though. Elisa was the other part, and *far* closer to home. Carter was hoping to win her over by having the production systems in place by the time she showed up...and maybe an informal offer of protection from Bethany Anne's wrath.

Secretly he kind of hoped the former Empress, now Queen, *did* show up. He'd heard her swearing could be really inventive when she got going, and he had always wanted to hear that. She'd chew Carter out, sure, but he'd get to meet one of his idols—and she might not destroy his *whole* stash.

For him, the risk just made it more fun.

The transport ship came down with a creak and a loud groan that made him wonder if it had really been wise to fly on it. Then there was the curious ear-popping sensation of an airlock opening. Even when it wasn't close, you could really feel it.

Carter shuffled along with the other people, marveling at how similar it was to airline travel. Everyone jumped up as soon as they could and grabbed for their bags, even though they knew they wouldn't get out soon.

To his surprise, though, there was no security check-point to go through. They just found themselves on a big, scorched pad of something like concrete with the city glimmering in the distance and a lot of vehicles nearby that were probably cabs.

Carter decided to walk. Most of the passengers seemed to be doing the same. The path was a swampy mess, but they hauled their bags along with grim determination—it looked grim to him, anyway—and he tramped behind them looking at anything and everything.

When he heard the distinctive whine in the air he looked around in absolute disbelief. It couldn't be. *Surely not.*

But it was. There were mosquitoes on this planet, or at least something like them.

Fucking unbelievable. He was going to try to contact the scientists on the *Meredith Reynolds*, because if anyone could whip up some effective bug repellant it would be them. And none of that DEET-free crap, either. He wanted the mosquitoes dead and the ground under them salted. Metaphorically, of course, unless literally salting the ground was what the situation called for.

You couldn't be too careful when it came to mosquitoes.

The city didn't begin gradually like he'd expected. The dirt road just turned into a paved one all at once, and suddenly there were buildings. Given that they had to take care not to sink into the swamp, Carter supposed that made sense.

He decided just to let the flow of people take him along for a while. He didn't know anyone here and it was morning, so he had plenty of time to find lodging. He could browse for a while and get a feel for the place.

A few people gave him long looks and he stared back equably. He didn't really mind that sort of thing. Humans were newcomers. Even on the *Meredith Reynolds,* people stared a lot. Carter had fielded a lot of questions about himself, from the ridiculous to the ridiculously personal.

After some wanderings between various stalls selling food that smelled pretty good but might not be safe, the crowd carried him to the edge of the street and he had a chance to look out over it all.

He liked this place; liked it instinctively. It was a bit rough around the edges, but in a homey way—like people who came here could put together their own stand to sell their wares, or build their own house, or start their own business.

He saw something that looked like a bar and forged across the street, ducking into the dim interior and stopping when he saw a monkey sitting there. It chittered at him.

His aural implant translated the words: "Good afternoon, human. Can I get you something to drink?"

"Yes, please." Carter heard the strange noises coming out of his mouth and shook his head slightly. It was weird using the implant. "Do you happen to know what's safe for humans to drink?"

He had same basic upgrades as the rest of *Meredith*'s population, but he didn't want to push it.

"I have fruit juice," the bartender told him. "The human who was here yesterday drank that with no problems." She added smugly, "He said it was very good. I make it myself."

"I'll have a glass of that then." Carter smiled at the weight of the Pepsi in his bag. Maybe he should see about setting up shop somewhere that was already established. It was something to think about.

In the meantime, he wondered if he knew the other human who'd been here.

Shinigami liked researching things.

To her knowledge, every computer intelligence did. The world seemed to be set up to disperse information at the pace organic life forms could take it in, which was far too slow for her. Researching allowed her to do something with all the time between words when people were speaking, and also for the interminable amounts of time in which they slept.

When she'd mentioned the latter to Barnabas, he had asked her whether she dreamt of electric sheep and wandered vaguely off again to plan his mission. So she kept researching.

It was galling to admit, but he'd made a good point the other day about viewing High Tortuga as a whole, not simply in the context of this one mission.

Where she differed from him, however, was that while he wanted to *talk* to people in order to find out what he should know, she was sure she could reach the conclusions far more efficiently by sifting through the data.

For a while she had looked at the ships going in and out of High Tortuga, noting the ships' makes and tracing their registrations. She'd made some progress, but not much. Not an awful lot happened here.

Then she realized that this was exactly the point—*not an awful lot happened on High Tortuga*.

What *did* happen here was, like the immigration of humans from the former Etheric Empire, the result of things happening elsewhere. The planet was simply a nexus where various forces and interests collided.

When she had realized that, her research had opened up significantly.

She went back through the records of the company that had owned the mines and compared High Tortuga to the other planets on which it operated. In not too long, she had found a simple but telling list of similarities: rich in ores, no indigenous sentient life, not wildly inhospitable, and most importantly, either not controlled by a government or very far from the government's central location.

This told her more about why people would look for a place like High Tortuga. They wanted somewhere that they could do exactly what they *had* done—put in a bunch of mines without having to bother about laws or land rights, and not spend a great deal of money keeping people in the appropriate atmosphere or pressure.

Once she saw High Tortuga as a planet possessing certain qualities, she began to understand who might want it. There were certain norms for who could own land on "unclaimed" planets, but those norms were often violated. There were also many people who *wanted* to live here, not so much to build businesses and grow rich as to exist without an entrenched bureaucratic government hanging over their heads.

From resources to a breakdown of certain types of settlers, Shinigami began to build a list of potential problem areas in keeping the planet safe.

That was not as interesting to her, however, as undoing what had already been done. She had been studying the behavior of sentient organic minds, and she was beginning to learn what some people called "tactics" and others called "sneakiness."

She had considered asking Barnabas for his input, but she was still not sure if ADAM and TOM had been serious about him being sneaky. She thought that might have been a practical joke.

In any case, she had a lot of ideas. She didn't need to involve him yet.

She found the scouting conglomerates that both sent their ships out into space to chart new planets and bought information from independent pilots. She had thought of simply erasing Devon from their databases, but that left the problem that another person would inevitably come along and sell the information again.

No, she needed to be sneakier. She worked her way into their systems and began to change Devon's classification. She couldn't simply say it was barren, since it clearly was not. Instead, she modified the information to say that there were severely hostile plant and animal life forms, possibly including indigenous sentient life, and that the original settlers had lasted just long enough to build fairly respectable-looking cities before being brutally killed off by the local animals and a host of nasty diseases.

The only alien life remaining on the planet, she put in there, was a series of fanatical cults that sacrificed new settlers and ate them, and most of them had likely been driven mad by disease.

As a finishing touch, she began to work on a program to make the automated scanning systems of ships—always on the lookout for a little extra cash by scouting habitable new planets—totally disregard Devon. *Nothing to see here, move along.*

She was just finishing up when Barnabas looked up from his reading material and asked suspiciously, "Shinigami, you've been awfully quiet. What are you up to?"

"How do you know I'm up to something?"

"Nathan and Ecaterina once mentioned that the most worrisome sound for the parents of a toddler is silence. I'm extrapolating."

"Are you saying that an AI is in any way comparable to a human toddler?"

"In *many* ways, actually." He sat back. "The main ones would be that it's too smart for its own good and also somewhat sociopathic. I believe the exact phrase Nathan used was, 'tiny terrorist.' You are basically a toddler with a flamethrower."

"Rude! Maybe I *won't* show you what I was working on."

"That suggests you were originally planning on doing so, which means you must have *wanted* to." He smiled.

"Maybe." But she brought up the charts and programs.

He leaned forward to scan through them, and she watched his eyebrows rise as he assessed the information.

"This is some very good work."

"Really?"

"Yes." He looked up at her sensors with another smile.

"You should add 'venereal' to the description of the diseases. Also, 'necrotic.'"

"Why? You don't think cerebral hemorrhage is good enough?"

"Trust me on this one, you want something visceral. And before you ask, no sentient life form is going to care as much about their brain as their... Well..."

"Why not? That doesn't make any sense."

"There's still so much you have to learn," Barnabas replied wearily. "Though for what it's worth, from a logical standpoint I agree with you."

"This is one of those times when organic life is illogical, then."

Barnabas snorted. "Sex? Yes, you could put it that way. It would be a massive understatement, of course, but it would technically be true."

"Hmm. I can probably use that in the future."

"You don't say." Barnabas stood up and carefully marked his place in his book. "Now, if you'll excuse me, I need to change."

"Why? Into what?"

"You'll see."

9

Barnabas walked slowly and meditatively as his steps carried him away from Tethra and into the mountains. He could walk faster if he wanted to. He could have run the whole way if he'd wanted to.

However, he had learned that the discipline of pacing himself allowed him to be more present in the moment. It was a ritual he had been taught as a monk, and he still practiced it at times.

Speaking of which...

This is easily the most ridiculous thing I've ever seen you do.

You've only worked with me for a week and a half. To paraphrase Eric, you haven't seen anything yet.

To paraphrase? What would he have said?

Barnabas wrinkled his nose slightly before repeating the exact phrasing. "*You ain't seen nothin' yet.*"

You really dislike poor grammar, huh?

Yes. It is an abomination. There are perfectly good reasons to—

This is gonna be sooooo fun.

I regret so many things right now. Barnabas drew back the cowl of his monk's robes and looked up at the mountains. *Shinigami, can you see this?*

Of course I can. Is that a joke?

No. Through my eyes, I mean.

Up in orbit, Shinigami paused in her research to look through Barnabas's eyes. She knew she had the capability to do so very easily if he wished her to, but it had never occurred to her that it would be useful.

She wasn't sure what she was looking at, though.

Look at the mountains, Barnabas told her. When she checked his heart rate, she found it to be unusually slow.

Is something wrong?

Precisely the opposite. This is beautiful. What you're seeing right now—things like this are why people travel and look for new places to live, even when it would be more difficult than living on a station like the Meredith Reynolds.

Shinigami assessed the image as well as she could. She still was not certain what Barnabas meant, but she sensed that there was something important about the exchange.

She filed away the logs to go over later.

So, are you ever going to explain to me why you're dressed like that?

Barnabas smiled as he began to walk again. The mine was not very far away. *Call it an indulgence. Missionaries tend to unsettle people. They also tend to be able to push situations further than someone in another social position. Simply put, this disguise will afford me opportunities I would not otherwise have.*

You're being sneaky. Shinigami was cautious in her assessment.

You could say that, I suppose.

You think they'll underestimate you, too, don't you?

Barnabas smiled again, and this time the smile was colder and harder. *Yes.*

Shinigami was silent as he climbed toward the gates, where guards waited in their towers. They watched curiously as he drew closer, and eventually the guard captain himself scrambled out to speak to this strange alien who was approaching on foot.

"This is private territory." His voice was uncertain. This person certainly didn't seem aggressive, and how could he possibly hope to do anything without any weapons? "I'm afraid I'll have to ask you to—"

"Good day to you, child." Barnabas gave his best monk's smile. He was bargaining that religious figures in alien societies spoke similarly. "I am Brother Barnabas, here to speak to Venfirdri Lan."

The captain drew up at the mention of his boss's name. "I... Is he expecting you?"

"No, child, he is not *expecting* me—but he does need to see me. I am here to bring peace to what may be a fraught situation." Barnabas smiled again and folded his hands in his sleeves.

And waited.

"I, uh... I'll, um..." The captain looked at Barnabas. He looked at the tower. He looked at Barnabas.

Barnabas kept smiling.

"I'll go see if he's available," the captain replied finally. "Would you like any refreshment, *Kalanon*?"

The term doesn't translate exactly, Shinigami told Barnabas before he could ask. *But it is a sort of religious figure in Brakalon society. I think it is a term of respect.*

Good.

Barnabas only shook his head. "I will wait here, child. Do not trouble yourself on my behalf. Go speak to the overseer, and I will await his response here."

"There's a *what* at the gates?" Lan looked irritably at the Brakalon. He could never remember this one's name.

"A *kalonon,* sir. A...speaker of words."

Lan blinked.

The Brakalon swung his head side to side in frustration. "A visionary. A person who sees truth and speaks it. We revere them above all."

"Let me get this straight: a Brakalon mystic has come to the gates and you think I should see them."

"Not a Brakalon, sir. I've never seen this kind of alien before."

"Then how do you know it's a—what was the word?"

"'*Kalanon,*' sir."

Lan prayed for patience. "That is not important right now. Shouldn't Venfaldri Gar be handling this?"

"Sir, the *kalanon* asked for you by name. It said that it was bringing peace to a fraught situation."

Lan pressed a button on his desk and waited. This conversation was getting him nowhere, and he was not going to waste any further time trying to explain that to his guard captain. When the door opened and Gar came in, Lan snapped, "What took you so long?"

"My apologies, Overseer Venfirdri." Gar bent his head.

"There's a religious...person...at the gates. Get rid of it."

At Gar's curious look, Lan added, "It's some type of alien no one has seen before."

A curious expression came over Gar's face and the vice overseer stepped politely around the Brakalon with a nod to him.

"A religious figure, you said?"

"Yes." Wearying of this conversation, Lan brought up the video from the gates—how did he do that again? Why was he being expected to do all this now?—and turned his computer screen.

"Ah," Gar said finally.

"Yes. 'Ah.' Get rid of it."

"Did he say why he's here, sir?"

To Lan's relief, since he was beginning to get quite annoyed with this relentless speculation, the guard captain answered, "He says he is here to bring peace to a fraught situation, Vice-Overseer. He asked to speak to Overseer Venfaldri by name."

Gar nodded contemplatively.

"Vice Overseer," Lan began dangerously, "if you value your job—"

Gar interrupted him, looking at the guard captain, "Captain, if you would give us a moment of privacy?" The captain nodded and withdrew, and Gar took a seat and leaned close to Lan. "With all due respect, sir, I think we might want to let the religious figure in."

"I assume that is a joke?"

"No, sir." Gar paused as if trying to think of the words. "You know, of course, that the workers are becoming...shall we say, 'difficult to control?'"

Lan sat in stony silence.

"Sometimes the distraction of religion provides the workers with a new place to put their energy—particularly if this is one of those religions that promises rewards for good behavior." Gar settled back in his seat with an inscrutable smile.

Lan's eyebrows rose. *That* was something he had not considered. "You think this *kalanon*—it's the term the Brakalon used—could be useful in settling the workers?"

"I think it is possible," Gar replied. He gave Lan a conspiratorial smile. "And if he is not, we can simply take care of it. After all, religious people like this tend to wander alone. It's likely no one knows where he is."

Lan chewed his lip. He was worried. "How did he *find* us?"

"That is another reason we should speak to him," Gar told him persuasively. "If there is someone in Tethra who knows the location of the mine, we need to know who." He added after a moment, "I was most careful never to leave any clues, and no one should have thought to follow me. I pretended to be a businessperson who had just arrived in town."

"That is good." Lan nodded absently, then shook his head slightly. "I'm not sure about this, however. You remember the Children of the Waves at home. They caused trouble. This one might do the same."

The Children of the Waves were a religious sect that Lan had always hated. Even before they bombed the walls of one of the submerged towers on Luvendan, sucking everyone within out into the waters to be devoured by nearby Essekan—the sect maddeningly believed this to be a sure ticket to heaven—Lan had hated them.

They were so self-assured, so sickeningly sweet. When you didn't take them seriously, they treated you as though you were too stupid to see the truth.

Lan had never trusted any religious figures on any planet since.

He was gratified that Gar seemed to take this concern seriously instead of brushing him off. Quietly Gar related, "You know, a lot of why I left was the Essekan. I knew they could crush the towers if they wanted—or even just my level, and I would be dead even if everyone else lived. I had terrible nightmares about it when I was little."

It wasn't a particularly unique nightmare. Every child on Luvendan had probably had it. Still, Lan felt a rush of companionship for this male. The memories of fear were incredibly strong, and Gar, like Lan, had left the planet.

"Why didn't they just leave?" Lan asked irritably.

Gar swallowed. "They were so content just to live in the dark in those towers. They should have wanted something better for their children. They should have wanted something better for *themselves*. Maybe the Children of the Waves—" He broke off.

"What?" Lan was curious.

"Maybe they did that because they were so afraid of the Essekan that they couldn't live with being afraid anymore. They wanted to get it over with." Gar's voice deepened, "It's difficult, waiting for death."

Lan blinked. The atmosphere in the room had grown abruptly dark, and he could not shake the feeling that Gar really knew what he was talking about.

But Gar shook himself and said simply, "In any case, the

scans there show that this alien has no weapons on him at all. And he looks small. Weak."

Lan nodded slightly, but he still was not sure.

"We should certainly not let him out among the workers," Gar added. "Not at once, anyway. But I think you should speak to him, Overseer. Perhaps he might have useful ideas, even if we decide not to keep him around."

It made sense, Lan had to admit. What was the harm in hearing the alien out? He'd been planning to spend the day watching one of his favorite shows, but he'd done that yesterday. And the day before. And the day before that. Much as he hated to admit it, he was getting bored.

Speaking to this alien would at least be something new.

"Captain." He waited for the Brakalon to push his head into the room. "Go get the alien. Bring him here."

Barnabas had wondered whether he would be able to fulfill his promise. Still, he was not precisely surprised when the gates swung open and the large alien beckoned him inside. The threat of imminent death seemed to spur creativity. Whatever Gar had said, it had plainly worked.

Shinigami, tell me about the layout while we walk.

You're at the eastern edge of the camp, by magnetic north. If you skirt the southern wall and then partway along the western wall, you will eventually come to a gate that leads to two huts on the hill.

Barnabas glanced in that direction. *The overseer's hut?*

It would seem so. The alien who is accompanying you went there and came back down.

Very well. What else? This place was depressing. Nestled as it was into a valley between the foothills of the mountain range, it somehow managed not to have an impressive view. Those who lived here would see only the grimy and dusty buildings and the heavy walls.

The place is set out roughly on a grid. There are many huts, of which I assume some are guard barracks and some are houses for the workers. If I had to guess, I would say the huts closer to the western gate are for the guards. This is assuming that many of them are Brakalon, because there are a few in those buildings right now. The other huts are to the east near the entrance to the mine. In the middle there are some buildings that might be a jail and a store and...I'm not sure what else.

Thank you, Shinigami.

Barnabas kept walking. The large alien at his side—a Brakalon, if he recalled correctly, which he almost always did—was treating him respectfully. He had scanned the guard's mind; he was in no danger from the male.

The Brakalon's large head—set forward on its shoulders compared to a human's, with a very short, thick neck —swung from side to side to better assess danger as he walked. His skin was remarkably pale, and warm-toned like a human's. His hands, meanwhile, had what appeared to be two fingers and a thumb, but with plates over the skin that seemed to be a part of it—perhaps similar to a fingernail?

Barnabas registered a strange mental presence and almost stopped walking, but he didn't want to be obvious. The Brakalon might be respectful, but Barnabas did not want to cause a scene...yet.

Still, he looked around curiously. The presence was

more like an absence; like a dark place where there *should* be something. He looked around, turning his head slowly so as not to attract attention, and saw an Ubuara peering at him.

He should be able to read this one's thoughts, but the radio chip that kept the Ubuara unable to communicate partially blocked him. The familiar anger surged within him, a slow burn that he knew would not stop until the situation was made right.

In the meantime, he stared into the creature's eyes and forged a connection using raw power. *Aebura has not forgotten you. I am here to help. Be patient. All will be made well.*

Then he turned his head away before the Brakalon could notice and followed him up the hill.

In the guard hut, Namlanor, one of the younger guards and thus always assigned to the boredom of electronics duty, heard a crazed beep-whistle from one of the devices. Swearing, he followed the noise until he came to the device that produced radio waves to silence the Ubuara.

He frowned. He didn't know how to fix this piece of equipment.

He thumped the top of it.

It immediately sank into quietness once more, all the dials indicating normal function.

Namlanor smiled and went back to his chair. Fixing electronics wasn't always complicated.

10

"So." Lan folded his hands and stared at the alien. He tried to think of something to say.

"How should we address you?" Gar asked diplomatically.

Lan gave him a slight nod to thank him for the question.

"Brother Barnabas, please." The alien looked between them. "I am guessing from your expressions that you have not met any humans before."

"Humans?" Lan considered. "No."

"We have only recently come to this sector of space," Barnabas told him. He smiled. "While we are newcomers, I believe we have much to offer, both in trade and in...other ways." He inclined his head. "That is why I am here."

"Yes. Explain that." Lan narrowed his double-pupiled eyes and considered this small and weak alien. Gar was right, it really did look quite useless. No wonder it had learned to rely on trade. "How did you know my name?"

Perhaps it was an information broker. If so, he would want to be even more careful what he said.

"When I landed here I decided to wander the countryside, and came upon your enclave."

"And again—how did you learn my name?"

Barnabas tapped behind his ear. "I have a device—a glorified database, really—that gives me answers to my questions. It told me that you had, at least at one time, been overseer here."

A "glorified database?" Do you *want to be the target for the flamethrower tests?*

Barnabas' lips twitched. He was enjoying Shinigami's tone, and he was also enjoying the look of worry on Lan's face as the Luvendi wondered just how many people knew where he was.

"Where did your device find that information? And how did you know we've been having troubles?"

"Ah, I should explain." Barnabas gave a self-deprecating smile. "I have simply learned that in places like this which are undergoing rapid expansion, things are always fraught. There is...progress, and at the same time, there are those who are not prepared to sacrifice to see that progress achieved. There can be a collision of people with different laws from different societies."

"Ah." Lan was put at ease by this. "I...see. Yes, you are correct. There are those here who do not understand progress. Who for some reason think that we should obey *their* laws."

"And?" Barnabas asked.

"Devon is a newly-settled planet, Brother Barnabas. It is not under the purview of any laws. Any claims made should surely be backed up before they are imposed, yes?"

Barnabas only smiled again.

He doesn't know how right he is.

Shinigami pointedly ignored him.

What if I let you use him *for flamethrower practice?*

I'll consider it. I assume you don't mean right now.

See, we're getting to know one another!

"Brother Barnabas." Gar spoke now. "How do you wish to, as you said, bring peace here?"

"Ah." Barnabas nodded at him. "You see, it is quite simple. Dissatisfaction comes from poorly-aligned expectations. Since you mention troubles and you are an overseer here, I will guess that you are having problems with the workers."

Lan nodded slightly.

"My guess is that the workers have expectations—the type of work they do, and so on—whereas you have different expectations."

"I do not have *expectations,* I have *facts,*" Lan shot back testily. "In order for the mine to function, work must be done. In order for it not to be bankrupted, the costs of food and lodging must be considered."

"They have not yet been persuaded to think this way?" Barnabas asked mildly.

"No." Lan knew he sounded somewhat like a sulky child, and he hated it.

"During my travels, I have found that I have a talent for aligning expectations," Barnabas offered.

And realigning spines, Shinigami added.

That as well.

"Brother Barnabas," Gar interjected, "while we do not wish to be disrespectful, I'm sure you can understand that allowing an unknown alien into this situation is a risk. What assurances can you offer us?"

Lan looked at him sharply, but he was pleased to see that this new alien did not seem to be insulted by the question.

"A good question. I beg your pardon, but I do not believe I know your name."

"I am Venfirdri Gar, vice-overseer of this mine."

"It is good to meet you, Vice-Overseer Venfirdri. You are, of course, wise to seek assurances." He paused for a moment. "What information would be of help to you as you make this decision?"

"Tell us about your religion," Gar suggested.

"Ah. Perhaps you are worried that I wish to set up some cult?"

"That *is* a concern," Lan agreed.

"I understand. However, that is not my reason for being here. I am not concerned with what gods you or your workers worship."

"'Gods?'" This was an unfamiliar term to Lan. Even Gar, the more well-read of the two, seemed lost.

The human seemed a little blindsided by this. "Ah. Hmm. A force beyond what we can see or measure. An ideal, perhaps. Something greater than mortal beings." When he saw their blank looks, he shook his head. "I am happy to speak to you about this, but it is not my purpose in being here. I wish only to restore peace to this place."

Lan came to a decision. "In that case, why doesn't Vice-

Overseer Venfirdri show you around?" His nod to Gar conveyed a silent warning: *Keep an eye on him.*

Gar nodded back slightly.

"I would be delighted. I sincerely hope I can be of use." Barnabas stood, and allowed Gar to lead him out of the overseer's hut.

Lan waited until they were gone, then hit a button to call one of the guards.

"Summon Chogaru."

He ate some sweets while he waited for the Nekubi to arrive. Gar had done well to bring them back. Such comforts were the only things that kept Lan sane in this miserable place while he accrued his money.

Still, there must be sacrifice in order to gain. If he had to live on this squalid planet for a few more years in order to become magnificently wealthy, he would do so.

He looked at the Nekubi as it slithered into the room.

At first, Lan had despaired of finding a way in which the Nekubi could be useful workers. With short weak arms and a bulbous body, they were not useful for many of the tasks normally performed in a mine.

However, the Nekubi possessed an unusual ability to find veins of ore and assess the quantity of it in a chunk of rock. Lan had been able to make excellent use of them.

Chogaru in particular had other uses. When he'd arrived, Lan had heard his name from the guards almost at once. He was a troublemaker, they said. He was seen whispering in corners with the other workers. Who could know what mischief he'd get up to?

Then something very unexpected had happened. Chogaru had asked to speak to Lan in the dead of night, and he had explained that he would be very useful to the overseer—for a price. He had established himself as one of the revolutionaries among the workers. Anyone looking to make trouble would come to him first.

He offered to be Lan's source amongst the workers.

Lan, who appreciated this sort of bargaining, had to admit that this was an unexpected bonus. He'd made sure to have the sort of delicacies Chogaru liked on hand for regular indulgence, including a certain sort of tree sap. He'd signed a contract offering Chogaru far more in the way of wages so that money would be waiting for him at the end of his year, and any month he stayed after that would earn him triple wages.

In return, Chogaru had made him aware of certain plans among the workers and advised Lan when to use force and when to capitulate to their demands. So far, Chogaru's advice had proved worthwhile.

Lan had not summoned him recently, however. He knew that Chogaru must have opinions on the tempers within the mines, and Lan had been afraid that the Nekubi might advise letting people out of their contracts.

"You have a problem, Overseer?" Chogaru dipped a finger in the tree sap and brought it to his mouth. The sticky stuff was just starting to drip as he licked it away.

"You tell me," Lan replied. "It's what I pay you for."

"You have several potential problems."

"Mmm. I'm aware of those. And there is now one more. Did you see the new alien walking with Gar?"

Chogaru shook his body in a way that Lan had come to interpret as a negative.

"He wears brown robes and is short, and has no claws or teeth to speak of. He is apparently a 'human.'"

"I've heard of humans," Chogaru related finally. "But they're myths; they don't exist. Whoever told you he was human was playing a prank on you."

"*He* told me he was human," Lan replied, annoyed.

"The stories about humans are impossible," Chogaru told him. "They say that humans can grow claws in an instant and battle creatures four times their size. Who has that kind of technology?"

"Kurtherians."

"Precisely. And what you described is not a Kurtherian." Chogaru rippled again; Lan thought this one might be a shrug. "So what do you want from me?"

"I want to know if this *thing* tries to make trouble or set up an insurrection; that sort of thing."

"Ah. If you're worried, why is he even here?"

"He claims he can help with the bad mood among the workers. It's worth a try. I'll just kill him if he doesn't help."

"Wise," Chogaru agreed. "Don't let it go too far. I'll see what I can find out about him."

Lan seemed to have nothing more to say, so Chogaru left with the Brakalon who had brought him here, pausing for restraints to be placed on his hands and tail. Whenever he came to speak to Lan, they pretended he was in trouble for some infraction or other. Chogaru told people this was why he'd stayed so long; Lan had extended his contract for all the trouble he'd made.

He didn't mind living here, not particularly. Ever since he could remember Chogaru had wanted *more*. More of anything, more of everything. At first he had despaired that a Nekubi from the lowest caste could ever rise in the world, but his instincts had told him to get off Nire, his home planet. Since he'd left, things had definitely been better.

Oh, there were problems. There were rough nights sleeping out in the open, or without food. But he was learning so much. He was learning how to trade what he had for something more, and he got better at it every time.

When he had run out of options on his last planet, he'd taken a contract with the company. He hadn't had any ideas of what to do when he was done with his year of work. He'd just known that it was better to go someplace new than get into a rut.

Once he'd gotten here, though, he'd seen the answer at once. Overseers were deathly afraid of insurrection, and it was all too easy to stir one up.

Lan thought Chogaru was on his side—and when push came to shove, maybe he was—but Chogaru wasn't useful unless there were workers' revolts to put down. Thus, he made sure to keep them going with a subtle word here, a little hint there. He was going to make as much of this situation as he could.

In this case, he had to admit he was curious. What sort of alien would dare try to pass themselves off as a mythical being? It was interesting, and it almost certainly meant there were secrets.

And if Chogaru had learned one thing over the years, it was that where there were secrets there was money to be made.

Barnabas walked through the dusty streets with his hands linked behind him and a carefully neutral expression on his face.

He'd decided to let Gar lead him wherever he wanted. There seemed to be good communication between him and the Luvendi. Barnabas had understood that when Gar asked for assurances, he was giving Barnabas the opportunity to set Lan's mind at ease. Gar had given faint nods when Barnabas had struck good notes, too.

Barnabas would therefore trust the vice-overseer to show him whatever he deemed useful, and only speak frankly when he knew they couldn't be overheard.

In the meantime, he was happy to have the opportunity to walk the layout of the town, seeing its weaknesses up close and assessing the mood in the workers. Many of them looked at him with scarcely-concealed dislike, assuming he was a friend of management because he was walking with Gar.

He would let them think that for now. It was extremely unlikely that any of them could hurt him badly enough to be more than an inconvenience, and they would know the truth soon enough.

He promised himself that.

Shinigami?

Yes?

Are you getting data?

Yes. She sounded pleased.

He was pleased as well. Before he left the *Meredith Reynolds,* he'd commissioned a series of pouches and pockets that went with various outfits. Though they appeared to be cloth, they were made of a fabric that resisted basic scanning technology, allowing him to stash various weapons and electronics in them.

In this case, secure in the knowledge that he could almost certainly keep fighting long enough to be picked up by a Pod, he hadn't bothered to bring weapons.

Instead, he'd brought a device that would find Lan's servers and feed information to Shinigami. While Barnabas was here, she would assess the data to see what they could find out about Lan and his employers.

He'd been impressed with her research about High Tortuga. She'd identified many places to tackle in order to make sure no one came looking for the planet—places Barnabas would no doubt have thought of eventually, but not soon, and not without carefully curated lists of exact cities and space stations where he might find relevant servers and information brokers.

He wondered how much else they could do if they set their minds to it. He had to admit, she'd gotten farther than he expected without speaking to people.

If only she weren't so damned impatient to use that flamethrower…

11

She should burn this whole place to the ground. Shinigami sorted through the files on Lan's computer, only growing more annoyed as she did so.

The company didn't care very much about its workers. A cursory check of their standard employment contract compared to any other employment contract revealed an eye-watering set of clauses that allowed for, as far as Shinigami could tell, things like having a relative work off any debt the company decided you had.

It wouldn't stand up in a court of law of course, but they were betting that no one they took would be able to get to one.

That would have been bad enough, but it was clear that Lan had cared even less about people than the company did from the start. The company had set an exceptionally low bar, and he had failed to meet it every time.

It was clear from the amount of food he'd requisitioned that he wasn't feeding the workers enough, and from his supply orders that he really only cared about his security systems and all the little luxuries he'd hidden under different line items.

He'd sent a message to the company to confirm that he would shut down the mines just as they had requested, then he'd taken everything offline and gambled that the owners wouldn't interfere—or, at least, wouldn't interfere for long enough that he'd be able to make a small fortune off the mine.

She wasn't sure if he'd planned to leave after a certain amount of time, or if he was only intending to run when he thought he was in danger. He seemed to be leaving his options open, even setting up a system of debts for lodging and food that would give him the chance to move workers somewhere else, claiming they still owed him money.

That was why you couldn't give people like this any indication that you were coming. Shinigami admitted to herself that she was worried—worried that Barnabas would not be sneaky enough and Venfaldri Lan would disappear with all his ill-gotten gains, and maybe even with some of the slave-workers.

The thought of someone getting away with this sickened her. The injustice of it was enough to make her want to climb out of her servers, take corporeal form, and do any number of violent things to everyone like Lan.

She could build herself a body if she had long enough.

Barnabas?

Yes?

Be honest: are you certain there is no room in your plan for Lan to escape?

His answer came back instantly: *Yes. I won't let him escape without paying for what he has done. More important, perhaps, is that I will never let him do anything like this again. The past cannot be undone, but the future can be shaped.*

Thank you, Shinigami replied simply.

There was a pause. She peeked through his eyes for just a moment and saw the world of the mines—depressing even to her AI eyes. Everything was shoddy and run-down. This place wasn't humming with activity or efficiency, and its denizens were not willingly laboring this hard. There was nothing to be proud of here beyond the grimly determined survival of the workers.

Were you worried? Barnabas asked her.

Yes. She did not see the point of the question. She would not have asked if she were not worried.

I am sorry, then, he replied at once. *It was not my intent for you to think that I...* He paused. *What* did *you think? To my knowledge, I have never given anyone in the former Etheric Empire cause to doubt my devotion to Justice.* He sounded offended now.

Not that, Shinigami told him. *I was worried that your pride was leading you to do this the difficult way for no good reason, and that Lan might have a chance to escape because of it. You cannot deny that humans do illogical things out of pride.*

As do AIs, Shinigami. All minds are prone to pride. It is, for all my jokes, one of the reasons it is good to work with a ship who can test my plans—and for you to work with a human who won't let you use that flamethrower without good reason.

Shinigami considered his words. *Maybe,* she agreed finally.

Maybe? Maybe? *You've been advocating charging in head-on when it might cost us months of time in finding others like this male, and—*

Got you.

A simmering sort of silence came through the ether, and Shinigami immersed herself once more in her research a bit hastily. She was incorporeal, so she wasn't precisely sure what Barnabas could do to make her sorry for her jokes.

She was, however, not stupid enough to find out.

Leiguba had not been hopeful when he'd seen the alien head up to the overseer's hut. Once—long ago—he had thought that aliens might come to help them. That they would see how Lan was running the place and report back to the company, and a better overseer would come.

He had learned that this was a foolish hope. No one cared. Whatever they might think when they saw the mines and its workers, nothing ever happened.

Maybe they even approved.

So when he looked at this one, it wasn't with anything more than bitter curiosity. The alien was dressed strangely, in long robes that looked impractical for manual labor and weren't of a very nice material.

But he seemed oddly dignified...and the guard captain treated him with respect, which was unusual. Even the guards didn't like Lan and Gar.

And then the alien had turned toward him and Leiguba had felt the thoughts pour in: *Aebura has not forgotten you. I am here to help. Be patient. All will be made well.* It sounded like someone yelling from very far away with their voice being drowned out by white noise, but Leiguba could hear it.

More than that, for just a moment, he could hear the frequency of the group mind. There wasn't anyone around who could share thoughts since all the other Ubuara still had working radio chips, but it was as if Leiguba'd had a head full of clouds and now it was clear again.

It was intoxicating. He stood staring after the alien and wondered what was happening.

Aebura has not forgotten you. Had Aebura truly sent this strange alien? If so, how did she propose to have him set the workers free? It had been so many months since she left. When the year was up and the overseer had refused to free them, Leiguba had been sure that Aebura would do something to release them.

But she hadn't. Locked in the mines, he couldn't tell if she even knew they were missing. He spent long nights torturing himself with possibilities. Had she left Devon behind, never even caring about them? Had she noticed they were gone and had gotten into trouble coming to get them? Maybe she'd forgotten the time passing and hadn't realized anything was wrong.

Now she had sent a single alien. Was she rich enough that she was sending a broker to buy the whole place?

I am here to help, the alien had said. *Be patient. All will be made well.* It sounded as if he was telling Leiguba not to do anything on his own, to just wait for things to happen.

But he could not keep this to himself. The workers here had been depressed and anxious for weeks, and he was afraid of what might happen if things got any worse. He saw the hopelessness in people's eyes. How long until they did something foolish, thinking they had nothing to lose?

He spread the word to the other Ubuara as best he could. Though they could not speak mind to mind now, they had noticed that the Brakalons could not interpret their native language very well. Sometimes they mistook it for just meaningless chittering, and that meant that they could pass messages.

Not only that, the Ubuara were used to passing messages. The links persisted, even when they could not connect to a group mind. Soon, the Ubuara were whispering messages to everyone they came across who was known to be friendly. *Help is on the way.*

It wasn't very far into the afternoon before Chogaru came to see Leiguba. Leiguba had been sitting in a patch of sun on one of the fences in a secret place that the guards didn't know about when Chogaru slithered into the alley.

"Do you know what these messages are all about?"

"Yes." Leiguba smiled. He was glad to see Chogaru. The Nekubi had been brave in standing up to Lan since he arrived, and he was always getting marched up to the overseer's hut and thrown into the little jail.

Chogaru was just the sort of person who might do something desperate if things didn't turn around soon.

"You don't need to worry anymore," Leiguba said. "Aebura has sent someone to help us."

"Aebura?" Chogaru looked doubtful.

Leiguba could not blame him, not particularly. Aebura had left soon after Chogaru arrived—back when Lan was still letting people go at the end of their yearly contract.

Chogaru didn't know her, so all the information he had was that she hadn't come to save them yet.

But now she *had*. Leiguba wrapped his tail around himself and tried to find a way to explain to the Nekubi why he was so sure this was going to work.

"This alien...he can override the radio chips," he told Chogaru earnestly. "That's how I know he's from Aebura. He looked at me, and for a moment I could hear the group mind."

"A hallucination," Chogaru replied dismissively.

Leiguba frowned. He understood not trusting Aebura, but this was different. Chogaru knew Leiguba. The Nekubi should know that he wouldn't lie about this.

"It wasn't a hallucination," he said firmly. "This alien is not an Ubuara, but he *can* speak mind to mind."

"Is this the alien who went to the overseer's hut?"

"Yes. You saw him?"

"He was coming down the hill when they brought me to speak with Lan." Chogaru flicked his tongue contemplatively at the corners of his mouth as if checking for any scraps of food that might have gotten away. "If he's talked to Lan and is still free to move around, clearly he isn't on our side. Has he done anything to prove who he's from?"

"No. Not yet." Leiguba's tail twitched. "We need to give him time."

"We might not *have* time."

"No." Leiguba got up and began to pace back and forth on the fence, using all four paws to walk. "We can't let anyone do something stupid. We were getting to the point where we might do something foolish. We need to wait and see what this alien does."

"And what if he's one of Lan's agents, trying to lure us into the open so they can crush everyone who wants to fight back?" When Leiguba looked stubborn, Chogaru folded his arms over his bulbous belly. "I think you're too quick to trust this human, just because he made you think something. Can't people lie mind to mind?"

"They...*can*," Leiguba said cautiously. "But it's awfully hard. Usually, when someone is doing a sneaky thing you can tell. The thought doesn't feel right."

"But it *is* possible."

"I suppose." Leiguba sat back down and rocked back and forth. "But then what do we do? Everyone knows he's here. I can't tell them he's *not* going to help us—especially when we don't know that for sure. That would be cruel, to take hope away without good reason."

"You *gave* them hope without good reason," Chogaru snapped.

"We haven't even talked to him! Maybe he'll have good answers."

"Maybe." Chogaru lifted a shoulder. "I'm not convinced."

"Come talk to him with me. Then maybe you will be." Leiguba frowned at the Nekubi and gave a little sigh of relief when Chogaru nodded grudgingly. "You won't regret this."

Chogaru still looked grumpy. "I still think we should organize on our own," he said after a moment. "They need to know we can fight back. They need to know we haven't forgotten what they're doing to us. And we shouldn't rely on outsiders. Why is Aebura sending someone after all this time, anyway? It's too weird."

"What if we fight back and we start something too big? We might get crushed. We can't fight Brakalons."

"You don't know that," Chogaru exclaimed. "We've learned all sorts of things about the guards. We might be able to pull it off."

"'Might?' We can't risk people unless we're sure!"

"Nothing is ever sure," Chogaru replied dismissively. "Now, are you going to show them that you're a force to be reckoned with or aren't you?"

Leiguba wavered. He would really rather wait to see what this human did. He'd trusted that human, even if he couldn't say why. He still thought the human was a good bet.

But maybe he was being foolish. Maybe he should trust Chogaru. After all, Chogaru was the one who *did* things. He was fearless, always getting hauled up to see Lan and always coming back to brag that Lan needed them more than he let on and the Luvendi was a coward.

Yes. He should listen to Chogaru. Chogaru knew what to do. Maybe if they were all brave like him, they'd already be free.

"Okay," Leiguba said. "Let's organize. Let's come up with a plan."

12

Shinigami was regretting her choices. She had agreed, much against her better judgment, to play chess with Barnabas again and had therefore used one of Barnabas's devices to project a chessboard and an image of Baba Yaga. Now, conscious of his reminders to behave like a human, she brushed a lock of white hair behind one ear and leaned forward to study the board.

"You're getting better at that." Given that she was using the device, Barnabas did not bother to use mind speech.

Shinigami did not respond. She was too busy thinking that this was another trap.

She couldn't have said why. He was playing far differently this time, moving pieces aggressively forward to get every game piece in play. His pawns were out, both knights were advancing, and he'd left a rook and a bishop in position to strike at her larger pieces if she dared move them.

It would be foolish of Barnabas to do the same thing again: play *not* to win.

But what if he was doing it anyway? It had been nonsensical the first time, too.

Hadn't it?

She hated humans, she thought grumpily. She hated them with every fiber of her being. Stupid, nonsensical, overly proud, illogical, absolutely untrustworthy, and they made bad jokes—and yet he'd talked her into playing him again. How had he done that? She should have known better.

She knew how he'd done it: she had wanted to prove she could beat him. She had come out of the last game feeling bamboozled. Feeling that he had won even though he had lost, and now she had to prove herself.

How did he *do* that?

"Your move," Barnabas reminded her mildly.

She raised her avatar's face to give him a glare and his lips twitched slightly.

He was mocking her. He was *mocking* her.

I will find a fitting way to make you sorry for this. Maybe I will lock you in a Sisyphean hell. Mind speech really was easier for her. Plus, she liked being the voice of God echoing in people's skulls.

Apparently he didn't. "That always sounded unpleasant." He looked at the roof of the cave contemplatively, as if admiring the sheer ambition of her goal. And then, uncannily sensing that she was ready to flip the chessboard and quit, he added, "If you don't want to play you could just concede."

Smug, self-centered bastard. She knew he had been manipulating her. She *knew* it.

And she still couldn't bear the idea of him wandering

around the ship, telling her he'd won both games, even if she knew it wasn't true. Oh, he was maddening. She was going to kill him in his sleep.

Wait, he didn't sleep.

No matter. She'd come up with something suitable. And then she'd kill ADAM and TOM for suggesting she work with him.

Thoughts of vengeance concluded, she moved one of her bishops into position to be captured, narrowing her eyes at him in challenge. *Come and get me.*

He moved a knight backward, staring her down with an evil grin.

Shinigami fought the urge to scream.

"I'm almost sure Lan is *not* part of a larger group," he remarked as he waited for her next move. "At least, per se. I think he has contacts in place to help him escape when he wants to, but I don't think there is any particular *set* of overseers who plan to break away."

Shinigami moved a pawn. What was the point of strategy when he was only going to lose on purpose again?

His words were hopeful, however. *Does this mean you're going to let me send a missile at that hut?*

"Not just yet. Be patient." He looked at the board, gave a minute shrug, and moved a knight.

Why wait? She moved another pawn. *I watched your physiological responses every time he talked. Your fingers were contracting. You wanted to strangle him.*

"I want to pull his spine out and strangle him with *that*," Barnabas corrected her in such a pleasant tone of voice that even Shinigami was a bit unnerved. "I'm waiting because I think if I can put him off-balance enough, he'll contact the various people who are willing to help someone like him...and who know about this planet. I don't just want to take out Lan, I want his whole network."

She gave the mental equivalent of a nod, then, *Someone's coming.*

Barnabas turned his head. "I hear them." His enhanced hearing had picked up the crunch of the feet of a bipedal being on gravel.

It's... Checking. It's the other Luvendi, Venfirdri Gar. She moved a piece.

"Interesting." Barnabas stayed hidden in the cave and moved a piece on the other side of the board that was manifestly unconnected to any of his previous moves.

Shinigami moved a mirroring piece—and realized her mistake when she saw Barnabas' lazy smile. He slid a rook down the side of the board. "Checkmate."

You have got *to be kidding me. You were playing to* win?

"Of course. It would be foolish to do the same thing twice in a row, don't you think?"

Then what was all that shrugging about?

"It's called 'bluffing,' my dear AI." He smiled at her as both the holograph and the game board flickered out of sight, and a moment later turned his head to look at Gar. "Hello."

Gar hesitated. "I came because... Well, is there anything I should be doing right now?"

Finding Lan's network and leading a coup? Shinigami suggested.

Unfortunately, he didn't realize for months what Lan had actually done. I'm not trusting him to do anything so complicated as figure the whole thing out.

Probably wise. You really are *an ass, you know.*

Barnabas smiled internally and nodded to Gar. "You are good to ask. As it happens, there is something I have not been able to determine yet, which is how Lan intends to get off-planet. He may not *have* a plan, but if he has one I want to know what it is."

Gar nodded. "And what are you going to do next?"

Don't answer that.

I'm not stupid, Shinigami.

"My plans are fluid, and they will remain private for now." Barnabas gave him a smile with just a hint of coldness to it.

Gar nodded nervously. "If you need me?"

"I will find a way to contact you." Barnabas knew his smile was not reassuring. He liked that in this case.

Gar was being useful, but he should not make the mistake of thinking he had nothing left to prove.

The Luvendi seemed to take this gracefully. He bowed and left with a murmured farewell.

Before you say anything, yes, I know I need to keep an eye on him. Barnabas glanced toward the ship in orbit.

Well, as long as you know.

I do. All right, I think I'm going to try to talk to the Huns next.

The...Huns?

The Nekubi. I was referring to the slug aliens from the Star Wars movies John and Bobcat like so much.

John says they're poorly acted and sloppy.

And yet he watches them once a month. What does that tell you?

That humans are maddeningly inconsistent?

117

Well, you're not wrong. Barnabas stood up and rotated his neck to work out a crick. *Once more into the breach.*

Chogaru watched Gar slowly make his way from the cave to the walls. The Luvendi had made a big show of examining the camp before he entered the cave, taking measurements and marking things on a map. Doubtless he would pretend that he had been assessing the defenses so he could make them stronger.

But Chogaru knew that the alien who called himself "Brother Barnabas" was in that cave right now.

He considered. He'd encouraged Leiguba to riot, thus ensuring that his place as an informant would be secure, but this was even better information.

If Gar were to be implicated, Chogaru might move up even farther in the hierarchy of the camp.

He just had to make sure Lan saw the evidence with his own eyes. But how to accomplish that?

"So, this is Pepsi?" Aebura stared doubtfully at the bubbly drink.

"Not so loud!" Carter looked around furtively. "No, this is Coke. This will be our official beverage, in accordance with the wishes of the Empress."

He pushed the beverage aside and laid out a brightly-colored sign, pitching his voice so other people in the bar could hear him.

"See? This sign shows that we make Coke, a beverage that is quickly becoming a favorite across the universe. It has a flavor that cannot be matched, and is the favorite beverage of the Empress."

"I thought you said the Etheric Empire had become part of a federation?"

"That's not as good for marketing. 'Empress' has a better ring to it."

"How is an empress different from a queen again?"

"It's... We're getting off into a weird area here. Just trust me on this one." Carter patted the sign again and projected his voice. "Yes, this poster certainly shows that we are devoted to the manufacture and distribution of Coca-Cola."

Aebura stared at him silently. He was behaving very oddly; she wondered if he was having some sort of health issue.

He leaned forward to whisper, *"Meanwhile,* we put out the word very quietly that true believers can get Pepsi here."

"Have I tried the Pepsi?"

"Yes. That was the first one you drank."

"I can't tell the difference."

If she'd been worried about Carter before, her concerns skyrocketed now. He stared at her, twitching vaguely, with his face going red.

He leaned finally closer and ground out in a sort of a strangled voice, "Listen carefully... That is *heresy.*"

The problem with humans, Aebura decided, was that you could never tell how serious they were. Sometimes when they were talking about very serious things, they would make jokes and understate the situation. Other times when the situation didn't seem to warrant it at all, they were very serious. Were they simply incapable of determining how serious things were in any normal way, or did they really consider the distinction between two nearly-identical drinks to be an issue of religious significance?

There was no way to tell.

She briefly considered fleeing the planet.

A moment later, she settled back on her haunches with a sigh. Humans, despite their flaws, were very useful and powerful.

Though she could think of no reason for a human to care about the mines, the one named Barnabas had seemed sincere when he'd told her he was going to help the mine workers, and he had indeed set off into the mountains where the mines might lie. He was putting his safety at risk for people he didn't know.

Perhaps she should indulge the humans' weird behavior —after a test, of course.

"Carter Eastbourne, how do you feel about slavery?"

Carter stood up very quickly and his face was very still, except for his eyes. He seemed to be trying to assess her mood.

"Why? Do slaves make your goods?"

"No. *No!*" She lashed her tail to add emphasis. "Never. I wish to know how *you* intend to produce this—and what you would do if you knew there were slaves nearby."

"I would send for backup from the Empire," he said at once. "There are people there whose task it is to handle those things." He squared his shoulders. "But if the Rangers couldn't get here, I would try to do something about it myself."

There it was. Humans were foolhardy, but they were foolhardy in pursuit of freedom.

"Tell me about the 'Rangers.'" It was a word she did not know.

"They travel alone—well, some of them—and when they see injustice they fight it. They are very strong fighters, and they are absolutely relentless when there are people being hurt. They're led by a human named Barnabas."

Aebura went still.

Barnabas was not simply a random human. He was one of the foremost humans, famous for his work in trying to gain Justice for the oppressed, and he had dedicated his life to this.

And he was helping *them*; people no one else had ever cared about before. She bowed her head and rocked back and forth.

"Aebura?" Carter sounded genuinely concerned. "Is something wrong? Do you need my help?"

"No. We'll be all right. Barnabas is helping us already. I just didn't know who he was until you said that." She ran her hands along her tail worriedly. "It is a very great honor. We are only a few people who signed contracts with the wrong company."

"If Barnabas has decided to help you, he has his reasons," Carter told her seriously. Then his eyes went wide. "He's not here right now, is he? Oh my God, he's standing right behind me, isn't he? He knows about the Pepsi. What have you done?"

"He's not right behind you," Aebura assured him.

"Oh, thank God. Why would you *scare* me like that?"

Aebura, who was not sure what she had done wrong, stayed silent.

"Listen," Carter continued seriously. "You absolutely must *not* tell Barnabas about the Pepsi."

Aebura narrowed her eyes. "You tell me that this Barnabas is a fighter for Justice, then you tell me to keep secrets from him? What is this Pepsi drink?"

Carter's eyes crinkled unexpectedly. "Think of this as a big prank members of the former Etheric Empire play on one another. Have you heard of Nathan Lowell, or perhaps Christina Bethany Anne Lowell?"

"The small child who can turn into a large canine fighter? Don't tell me she's *real*."

"Oh, she is. Nathan is a…well, it's a long story. Suffice it to say, he is one of the Empress' closest friends, which is why his daughter shares her name. He has also set up secret facilities to make and distribute Pepsi. We might have some fights about it—really, I might get my ass handed to me—but this isn't an issue of Justice." He got a distant look in his eyes. "Or perhaps it is. Justice for the oppressed Pepsi drinkers of the world."

She still couldn't tell if he was being serious, but she thought he was telling the truth about this not being an issue of Justice. She made a mental note to ask Barnabas about Pepsi in a roundabout sort of way the next time she saw him and snuck sips of the two beverages.

Apparently she was going to have to learn the difference between them.

G ar walked at what he hoped was a normal pace. He wasn't very good at deception. Even when he had cared about his own ambitions above everything else, he'd been honest about it. He had never been the person listening to everyone's secrets and blackmailing them later, and he didn't tell lies.

This all felt very odd.

The thing was, he hadn't gone to the cave in an effort to save his own skin. Clearly the human believed that was why he had been there, but the truth was stranger than that. Gar had gone because he wanted to do *more*. After months of doing things that felt wrong—making things worse and punishing people in ways they didn't always deserve—this felt like undoing all that.

He resisted the urge to go back to the cave and explain this to Barnabas, but he knew the human wouldn't believe him. What reason did he have to do so?

In the end, Gar decided. In the end, after he had done what Barnabas asked, *then* the Ranger might believe him.

He busied himself with menial tasks that gave him a clear view of the overseer's hut. Lan had recently decided to inspect the jails. He was worried about an uprising, and not without reason. He was getting paranoid.

Once he left, Gar intended to go look around and see if he could find Lan's contact for getting off-planet. Lan was lazy. He wouldn't have memorized the long strings of digits necessary for interplanetary communications. He'd have written it all down somewhere.

Gar wrinkled his nose. Lan had probably hidden things somewhere he thought was very clever, but really wasn't.

When he saw Lan head down from the hut, he had to stop himself from rushing up the hill. Instead, he waited while Lan came into the square and stopped to talk with him.

"What are you doing this morning?" Lan asked abruptly. He was trying to appear as if he cared about the day-to-day operations of this place.

If he had cared, he would already know Gar's usual tasks.

"I'll be doing an inventory of the food," Gar lied. "I think someone is stealing rations. I need to confirm the totals of every category." It would be clear even to someone unfamiliar with the daily jobs that this task would take a very long time. Lan would not think it odd for Gar still to be working when he got back.

"Very well," Lan replied and left, puffing his chest out self-importantly.

Once he was gone, Gar headed up the hill. He took care not to look around too much, and at the door to Lan's hut he smiled at the guards. "Lan sent me to look for a contract."

Bored, they waved him inside. They knew he was the one who did the work around here. This way they wouldn't be confused if they came in and he was looking through the paperwork. He even had his excuse ready. *None of this is filed in any sort of order.* They'd believe it; he knew they would.

Down in the town square, Chogaru saw Gar disappear into the hut. Then, in a calculated move, he picked up a rock and threw it through one of the windows of the commissary.

"This is an outrage! The overseer goes to inspect the jail while we starve!"

The Brakalons nearby sighed deeply before restraining him and hauling him into the jail, while Chogaru howled dramatic things about how he would say all this directly to Lan's face. He wasn't afraid. He was fighting for justice.

Inside, Lan heard the commotion and frowned. He had learned to take Chogaru's complaints very seriously.

"We'll take care of it, sir," one of the Brakalons informed him respectfully.

"No," Lan snapped. "I'll handle it myself." He watched while they hauled Chogaru into one of the far cells and chained him to the bars, then Lan leaned forward to hiss, "What is this about? Is this about the person stealing food? I knew about that already."

Chogaru paused, surprised. "Who's stealing food?"

"Gar told me about it." Lan gestured impatiently. "I assumed that was why you were talking about starving."

"I'm talking about starving because you don't feed us enough," Chogaru replied.

Lan frowned. The Nekubi really was pushing his luck these days by being very disrespectful. He'd have to do something about that soon.

"*That's* not why I wanted to see you," Chogaru clarified. "Gar is betraying you."

"What?" Lan laughed and shook his head. "No, he isn't. He's—"

"In your hut right now, after having gone to a cave to speak secretly with the so-called human." Chogaru smiled slightly. "Go check. You will see what you will see. What his plan is, I don't know—unless *you* sent him to speak with this 'Brother Barnabas.'"

Lan swallowed, then he whirled around and left. Chogaru was still chained to the bars.

Chogaru sighed without any real frustration. A few minutes, even a few hours, chained to these bars would be no trouble if they gave him Gar's job.

The others, of course, would be furious when they knew what he had done, but there were ways to blunt that. Chogaru would recommend that the bravest ones be killed. That way, no one else would dare rise up.

He settled against the bars to wait.

Lan's hearts were pounding as he scrambled up the hill. Gar? Betraying him? *Gar,* who was so careful to be logical and—

Of course. He had learned about the mines being turned over and he hadn't understood. He'd wanted the whole thing for himself. That must be what this was. He was trying to figure out Lan's secrets so that he could run things.

Lan would make him very sorry he'd tried.

It was still worrisome. He would not have suspected Gar; he thought he'd known the male. He had never seen Gar do anything deceitful. How could he have been so wrong? Part of him hoped that Chogaru was lying.

He burst into the hut without warning and scowled when he saw that his worst fears were true. Gar was here, surrounded by private papers that Lan had kept in a safe. How had he known the combination?

Lan must have entered it at some point while Gar was there, never dreaming that his vice-overseer would betray him like this.

"I suppose you have a good explanation." His voice was ugly.

"I couldn't find the shipping records," Gar replied after a moment. "I didn't want to trouble you, and you've used the safe while I was around. I didn't think this would bother you."

It was a plausible answer; almost plausible *enough*. But he'd never seen Gar like this, white-faced, with his hands shaking slightly.

And Gar slipped up even more when he asked, "Who told you I was here?"

Lan pulled out a pistol. "*That* is none of your business, just like these papers are none of your business. What are you really looking for?" He could see Gar sorting through different explanations in his head to find something believable and he shook the weapon threateningly. "Don't lie to me! I know you're working with the alien!"

Gar swallowed and tried to think of something to say. He had been so careful, making sure that none of the guards saw him going to the cave. Who could have told Lan he was there? Who could possibly know?

What sort of story would Lan believe now? Should Gar tell the truth?

A strange sort of clarity came over him at that thought. It did not matter what he did, as long as he did not let Lan suspect what the monk planned.

"I don't know why you would think I am working with the monk," he replied finally, trying to look as puzzled as possible. "I am trying to think of what I could do that would make you think that."

"You went to the cave to speak with him," Lan accused, tight-lipped with annoyance.

"I didn't go to the cave to speak with *him*, I went that way to survey the walls." Gar withdrew a map from where it was rolled at his belt and passed it to Lan. "See? If you were to go there and look you would note the same weaknesses. While I was there, I heard a noise and saw the monk in the cave. He said he was meditating, so I left him there."

Lan hesitated. He was not sure what to think of this. When Gar spoke of the map—which was something that could be verified, of course—his face had been shining with honesty. And he *had* been reviewing the various defenses. He'd told Lan that yesterday.

"Then why are you here?" he asked finally.

Gar hung his head. "Exactly why you'd think. Well, apparently you think I'm working with this alien, and that's not it. But what would you have thought if the alien weren't here?"

"That you're looking to take over from me," Lan hissed. "That you're going to kill me and run the mine, yourself."

"No!" Gar looked horrified. "I just wanted my fair share. I thought you were cheating me!"

Lan blinked. He *had* thought about permutations of that while he'd walked up the hill.

"And it's bad business," Gar continued. "I know the workings of this camp. I work hard. I have kept your secrets about...." He lowered his voice, flicking his eyes toward the door where the guards were posted. "I have kept your secrets," he continued finally. "I waited for you to offer me more, as you should have. I hoped that my offer of loyalty the other day would be understood, but instead you insulted me. So I wondered, why would Lan do this? Is the mine doing poorly, and he does not want me to know? But no!" He shook the piece of paper he held. "The mine is doing well! Profits have never been higher! And you cheat me!"

For a moment, Lan felt a pang of guilt and indecision.

Gar might deserve more of a share, but he had now shown that he was willing to be trouble, to bide his time and strike unexpectedly after pretending to be content. Lan couldn't trust Gar anymore, nor could he let this story get away from him. What happened to Gar had to be indisputable, so it had to be public.

"Guards!"

They appeared at once and looked surprised to see Lan pointing a gun at Gar. "Yes, sir?" one of them asked politely.

"Take Venfirdri Gar away." Lan deliberately did not use the Luvendi's title. "He is trying to take the camp over by force. Put him in the jail while I decide how to punish him."

He stood back and let them drag Gar away. The other Luvendi seemed dumbstruck.

At least he wasn't pleading for mercy. That would have been tiresome. Lan watched the figures for a moment from the doorway, then slammed the door behind him.

What had he ever done to deserve this sort of betrayal?

In his cave, Barnabas sat back with a contemplative expression on his face. Shinigami had made him aware of the argument and fed the audio into Barnabas's aural implant.

Where is Gar? he asked her.

He is being brought to the jail.

Strange. I would have guessed that Lan would just kill him.

It is unexpected, she agreed. *Perhaps we have underestimated him. I thought he had no self-control at all.*

He's like any cornered animal. Barnabas chewed his lip. *He's dangerous because he's desperate. He knows that if he doesn't make Gar suffer in public, people will think he's weak. He wants them to see it in gory detail.*

So what are you going to do?

I'm going to move the plan up. I'll check back in with Aebura to find out where the best hiding places would be, then I'll come back to the ship to gear up.

What about Gar?

Barnabas hesitated. *I will save Gar if I can. He did not tell Lan about our plans even when he might have easily become a double agent—and he had no way to know we could hear him. I almost wonder if he's had a moral epiphany. But he has also done very grave wrongs and participated in slavery. Death would be a fitting punishment. I will save the slaves first, and him only if it does not endanger the rest of them.*

He sensed her approval. *Do you want a Pod?*

Yes. Thank you, Shinigami.

Down in the town, Leiguba watched as Gar was dragged into the jail. He had been at Chogaru's window, trying to reassure him. It was really very frustrating how Chogaru started these disturbances with no plan, but Leiguba could appreciate his frustration.

Chogaru heard the commotion and asked Leiguba, "What has happened?"

"Venfirdri Gar has been arrested," Leiguba replied, surprised. "Why, I wonder?"

"*I* know," Chogaru told him sagely. "I saw him go to a mountain cave where the human was hiding. Perhaps they're plotting together." He sounded smug. "I told you the human couldn't be trusted."

"If Lan doesn't like him, then he must be our ally," Leiguba protested.

Chogaru sighed. "You think so simply. The powerful people struggle amongst themselves without caring about us. This fight is about power, mark my words. Lan and Gar both want to run the mine, and Gar lost. I'll bet he was the one who really brought the human."

Leiguba knew it was useless to argue with him since

Chogaru was very stubborn, so he nodded and pretended to agree.

"I'll bring you food later," he told the Nekubi and scampered up the roof to hide in the shadow of the chimney.

He didn't like Gar very much, but what if Gar *was* working with the human?

If he was, he might be a valuable ally. He would have to figure out how to use this information—and how to determine Gar's allegiance.

14

When Barnabas walked into Aebura's bar again—try as he might, he couldn't make out any meaning from the marks on the sign—she looked pleased to see him.

"Hello, Ranger Barnabas. Wait here and I will get you some juice." She raced off and came back quickly with a glass of juice held carefully in her hind feet.

Now she's calling me "Ranger." I need a new title.

You said it didn't need to be at the top of the to-do list. We've been kind of busy, you know.

Barnabas did not answer, instead reaching out to take the glass of juice. He took a sip. "Thank you. This is delicious, as always." He knew she enjoyed being complimented on it, and he was happy to see her smile. She gave a little shiver of fur that he interpreted as happiness, which was confirmed a split-second later when he felt the faint brush of her mind.

He did not say anything in response. He did not want to surprise her by letting her know that he could see into the group mind. If he did so later, he could pretend that it was an acquired skill.

"You remember that I promised to ask for your help if I needed it?" Barnabas asked seriously. "I think I need some help now."

Aebura was both pleased and worried. A few days ago, in a moment of emotion, she had been ready to race off at once and attack Venfaldri Lan with her bare hands. Since then, however, and especially since learning who Barnabas really was, she had realized that would be foolish.

What did it mean that he wanted her help now?

"I only need information," Barnabas told her. He could see Aebura's concern and reassured her. "About the mine."

"Oh. What do you need to know?"

"Are there any places where people like to hide? Places where the guards wouldn't think to look, *and* where they'd be safe from bullets. The bullets are actually the important thing. I hope to have the rest of it wrapped up quite quickly."

Aebura considered this.

"Maybe inside the mine," she dubiously replied. "There are places by the walls, but they don't have enough space for a lot of people. One person could hide there if no one saw where they went. And the huts are so shoddy that bullets would go right through them. But the mines are up the hill, so if everyone ran to the mines at once…"

"Hmm. Actually, that gives me an idea. If I were to attack during the day everyone would be in the mines already, right?"

Aebura shook her head. "I can't be sure. Lan was always saying that we should have multiple shifts so the mines were never closed." She frowned. "I'll bet he's made people's hours longer, too."

"That sounds like him," Barnabas agreed. "Frankly, I'm surprised no one has assassinated him yet."

I'm not. What would happen after?

One of the guards could have done it, Barnabas pointed out. *They clearly don't like him much.*

Oh, I hadn't thought of that.

"Sometimes I thought Gar might," Aebura mused. "He is a very ambitious male, that one. He doesn't let anything stand in the way when he wants something. You're *sure* you trust him?"

"I *was*," Barnabas replied. "In a very limited capacity, mind you. But now with so many people asking, one *does* wonder. I *will* say, he has gone out of his way to protect my interests even when it wasn't in *his* interest to do so. Lan had him arrested just before I came here."

"Why?" Aebura asked.

"He was looking through Lan's papers for off-planet contacts. I asked him to do so. When Lan caught him he lied and said he was looking for proof of profits so he could negotiate a raise."

Aebura considered this. "He could have been doing both."

"Why not sell me out, though?" Barnabas pressed.

"I just know I don't trust him," Aebura stated, her tail lashing.

She's not wrong to hate him, Shinigami pointed out.

I know. I only expected him to do the bare minimum and no more. Shinigami, I of all people know what it is to regret my past.

The AI had no quick retort.

Meanwhile, Barnabas assured Aebura, "The workers are my first priority. I will make sure all of them are freed and safe before devoting any attention to Gar."

She nodded, pleased.

"I will be moving very soon," Barnabas told her. "And I wanted to pass along that I saw Leiguba very briefly, right when I got to the camp. He looked well."

"How did you know it was him?"

Now Barnabas was in a sticky situation, and he had no choice but to confess, "I did not tell you, but I have some skills at mind speech. I was able to ascertain who he was, so I passed a message to him that you had not forgotten him and that I would help. I was able to override the implant for only a moment, but I'm very sure he heard me."

"Thank you, thank you." Aebura chittered as she swayed. "I am so grateful, Ranger Barnabas."

"Why are you calling me that?" Barnabas asked her curiously. "You do not need to use my... Well, my former title."

Aebura decided to tell him the truth, or most of it. "Another human came in here. He mentioned the Rangers and your name. He was most impressed by your abilities and honor."

Barnabas smiled, but it seemed a bit distant to Aebura. "I hope to make this planet safe in time for the settlers who get here. They are counting on me." He stood. "I must go. Be well, Aebura. I hope to be back with good news very soon."

"Barnabas?"

Barnabas turned with a smile. "Yes, Aebura?"

"What is 'Pepsi?' Is it a matter of honor? Is it a kind of injustice?"

To her surprise and relief, Barnabas began to laugh. He held his sides and doubled over, gasping for air. Finally he stood up and wiped his eyes. "Oh, my. I see you weren't joking when you said members of the former Etheric Empire had been here. Pepsi is... No, it's not a matter of honor or injustice, it's just a drink." He blinked one eyelid shut at her. "But if you ever meet the Empress, *don't* tell her I said that. She takes the supremacy of Coca-Cola very seriously."

He was still chuckling to himself when he disappeared, and Aebura stared after him with her head tilted to the side curiously. She was reassured, but even *more* certain now that humans took very strange things seriously.

She wrinkled her nose. After all, it wasn't like this was the debate between *hakoj* juice and *iterze* juice. This was just a silly argument about something that didn't matter at all.

Lan paced around his little hut.

The papers had been shoved back into the safe unorganized and threatened to spill out while he slammed the door shut. He couldn't look at them. Just seeing them—seeing all the evidence—made him want to burn everything.

Was it time to leave?

He had hoped to have a few years here to build up a good nest egg. He didn't like being here, but he wanted to get all he could while he could. Another opportunity like this was unlikely to fall into his lap any time soon.

He should never have sent Gar to the city. At the time he'd thought there was no one he could trust quite so well, and he was also afraid that the vice-overseer would take over if he himself left, but maybe Lan *should* have gone himself. He could just have run away entirely if Gar had taken over, and if he had?

If he had, Gar wouldn't know about the mines being shut down. Lan was sure now that Gar had really learned about everything on the trip, no matter how he'd played it off. He'd been frustrated before he went to Tethra, but he hadn't displayed any signs of wanting a bigger share.

Until the other day. Lan shot a resentful look in the direction of the jail. He would have given Gar something for his trouble. He would even have taken him along when it was time to go.

Or would he? He confronted the guilty thought that he had chosen *not* to offer Gar more money.

No, he wouldn't have helped Gar. In reality, he'd been planning to alter the records so it looked like Gar had always been in charge. By the time Gar convinced them of the truth, Lan would have been long gone.

On some level, Gar must have figured that out.

Well, he wouldn't be any more trouble. He was locked up in the jail and—

And what if he told people the truth? Lan ran to the radio and paged the guard captain. The minutes before he appeared were agonizing.

"How is Venfirdri Gar?" Lan asked abruptly.

"I have heard no reports from the jail, sir." The captain

looked wary. "I assume all is well. We put him in the new building alone, sir. We didn't want you to think we were coddling him, but you said you wanted to deal with him yourself. We thought the other prisoners might hurt him."

Lan sank into a chair, shoulders sagging with relief. Gar didn't have anyone to talk to. That was good.

"I want him totally alone," he told the captain. Hopefully the male would think this was just a punishment, so he added, "Just him and his thoughts. No distractions."

"Of course, sir. I'll have the guards stationed outside."

"Thank you, Captain. You may go."

Lan tapped his fingers on the desk as he considered what to do next. He should just leave tonight. He should call for a flight out of Tethra and slip away while everyone was waiting for him to make a decision about Gar. It would be the safest thing to do.

But he didn't want to give this up...not yet.

The little voice in his head that had told him to take the mine's radios down was now telling him not to walk away while there was still profit to be had. An opportunity like this only came along once or twice in a lifetime, it said, and reminded him that there was no gain without risk.

Which meant that he needed to make a different call.

He opened a channel to one of his contacts in Tethra, an old Brakalon who was unusually pragmatic compared to the other Brakalons Lan had met over the years.

"*What is it?*" His voice was grumpy when he answered.

"I want to purchase your services," Lan told him simply. He avoided specifics and didn't use the word *need*. He wasn't going to let Jutkelon hear weakness. He tried to sound bored. "Some of the workers think they can be clever and break out. I want to show them that the guards they see aren't the only things they have to contend with."

"Ah," Jutkelon replied contemplatively. "A wise strategy. A show of force can be very effective, but not all of my clients understand that."

Lan smiled thinly and did not respond to the compliment. He was used to salespersons trying to flatter him. "How much?"

"How many do you want?"

"You know how many workers and guards we have. Tell me what you think I'll need and I'll consider it."

Jutkelon laughed a little under his breath, but after a moment of humming and grumbling to himself he produced a number that Lan found surprisingly reasonable.

"Done," Lan confirmed promptly.

"You want them at the mine?"

"No. I'll send you details."

Lan cut the call with the appropriate pleasantries—so tedious, but Jutkelon was a resource to be cultivated—and considered.

No. He was not willing to leave just yet. This was *his* mine. He'd staked his claim, and he was going to keep it. *Let them try to take it.* He had dozens of guards, and really— what could one tiny alien do against dozens of guards?

15

Gar sat alone in his cell and faced the unpleasant realization that he was the weak link in everyone's plans, and therefore almost indisputably expendable.

He would say he wasn't sure where he'd gone wrong, but that wasn't true. He could think of any number of places. The first was when he'd strode confidently into the company offices on Tedrift Station, determined to get a job no matter what it was. The second was when he'd begun following Lan's lead a few months back.

The third, unfortunately, was when he had joined up with Barnabas.

The facts spoke for themselves. The way Gar saw it, he should have chosen one or the other. If he had stuck with Lan, the two of them might have been able to kill Barnabas. For instance, he could have hit the human with cannon fire the second he walked through the gates. Maybe they could have put poison into his drink.

Had anyone remotely familiar with the Etheric Empire

been around at this point and privy to Gar's thoughts, they could have told him how wrong he was.

Yes, as far as Gar was concerned, he'd messed up by picking both sides. He should have chosen one side and stuck to it. That would have been the best way not to end up a bloody smear on the wall.

He was still considering this when one of the Ubuara slipped through the window of his cell and dropped to the floor. It chittered at him in its own language for a moment in the way they started conversations.

Then, "I am Leiguba."

Gar stared at him suspiciously. What would this Ubuara want? To get back at him for so many years of mistreatment? That made undeniable sense.

"Why were you arrested?" the Ubuara asked.

Gar gave a bitter laugh. "I worked for the human you saw in the town the other day. Lan caught me, and now I am here."

"Why did you work for the human?" Leiguba asked him.

He was genuinely curious. When Chogaru had told him the reason for Gar's arrest Leiguba had not believed him. Never once in his time here had Leiguba seen Gar show any consideration for anyone else. Since the Ubuara believed absolutely that Barnabas was here to help them, that meant Gar was not working for him. If anything, Leiguba had come here to prove that Chogaru had been wrong.

Now it seemed the Nekubi had been wrong about everything.

"I wanted to save my own skin," Gar replied. He lifted

his thin Luvendi shoulders in a hopeless shrug. "Everything you have heard about humans is true."

"I've never heard *anything* about humans. They can talk mind to mind, you know."

"They can?" Gar briefly looked interested, then lapsed back into despair. "I suppose nothing about them would surprise me at this point. He can run impossibly fast for his height. His eyes glow red."

Leiguba stared at him, wide-eyed.

"So when he confronted me, I made a bargain," Gar said. "I dressed it up nicely for myself. I told myself I was becoming a better person; that I wanted to help him because it was the right thing to do. I told myself I wanted to prove myself to him so that he would include me in other things he had planned."

"It was not true?"

"No. I only wanted to save my own life. I was a coward. He told me that the punishment for my crime was death and I tried to be brave, but I was afraid to die. I can see now that I would have said anything, believed anything, to survive." Gar looked at Leiguba.

Leiguba tried not to shudder. Luvendi were difficult to look at. Everyone knew they had two hearts, and they had two pupils in their eyes too. People shied away from Luvendi because those eyes were so hard to look at. They looked *wrong*.

Gar's were even weirder than most, in that the color around the pupils was brighter than normal for a Luvendi. It was a bright blue-green that was remarkable to any alien species looking at it. The workers had all discussed this.

When you had to stare at his strange eyes you wanted to rub your own.

So Leiguba tried to think of something to say to distract himself.

"Wouldn't it have been easier to tell Lan what was going on? He can call on many guards. Surely Barnabas couldn't take them all on."

Gar smiled again, although he still looked bitter. "Yes, in hindsight it's clear. At the time…"

Leiguba did not let him get out of answering. "At the time?" he asked pointedly.

"At the time I thought I was a better person than I have turned out to be," Gar declared flatly.

"I do not understand why fearing death would make you a bad person," Leiguba told him. "We do not want to die either. It is why we do not simply rise up and fight the guards. It is why there *are* guards. Most people fear death. I have seen you exhibit many poor qualities during my time here, but not cowardice."

Gar stared at him intently. "Why are you here, Ubuara?"

"'Leiguba.' I am here to help you. You helped Barnabas, and it is possible that you could help him even more if you were to get out of here."

Gar stared at him, those strange pupils glittering in the darkness. "It would be unwise," he admitted finally, "to trust me."

"I know," Leiguba agreed. "But I will do it anyway."

"Why?"

"Because… No, I do not need to tell you why." The truth was, Leiguba knew he had no reason to trust Gar. The Luvendi was right.

But he was going to do so anyway. He had made up his mind when he'd come here.

Anyway, what was the worst he could do now?

Leiguba leaned forward. "Listen closely. In two minutes your door will open, and you must go out the back entrance of the hut. I'll distract the guards. When you get out, you'll…"

Lan looked at the group of mercenaries and gave a pleased nod. They were a variety of species: mostly Brakalons, but there were even a few Shrillexians. They would be especially useful for this show of force.

The group stood at attention in the road wearing basic uniforms—just brown pants and a shirt, but in Lan's experience, even *that* was unusual in mercenary companies. Out here, where there were not many luxuries or standards, any person with a gun could hire themselves out as a mercenary.

Jutkelon had higher standards, and he'd trained them all well. Each had a weapon which was clearly well-used and regularly cleaned, and they did not mill around or look contemptuously at Lan.

"They will take your orders," Jutkelon told him without a hint of evasiveness in his voice. "You don't need to worry. I've culled those who were cowards, or thought they should be giving the orders."

It was clear from his tone just how he'd culled them, and Lan smiled in appreciation. Too few leaders these days seemed to be willing to do what must be done, and too many tolerated people asking questions.

Perhaps he should take Jutkelon with him when he left, but he had the suspicion that the Brakalon would want to stay here and take any contracts he chose, not be tied to one client. On a planet growing as rapidly as Devon, there would be too many opportunities for someone like Jutkelon to pass them up.

"What's your plan?" Jutkelon asked now. "You tell me, and I'll communicate it to them."

The mercenaries were still waiting in the road for the two males to finish their conversation, but they did not fidget. Lan knew this was just advertising, but he was still pleased by it. Discipline in a soldier was a good thing.

"The camp is roughly square," Lan told him. "I want guards surrounding every building and all around the walls so that no one thinks they can sneak anywhere. We want them in alleys, at the entrances to the mine... anywhere they *should* be. If there's a confrontation, that is. They might just be stupid enough to try that."

"Hmmm." Jutkelon considered. "So the goal is to have a clear presence and rapid response if necessary." He handed Lan his staff and pointed to the dirt road. "Draw me a map of the town and mark the guard towers."

Lan drew, glad that he did not need to touch the ground. He hated the dust in the mountains, but the swamp surrounding Tethra was even worse.

He was not going to miss this place when it came time to leave.

Jutkelon watched the drawing take shape, and then he looked at the assembled group and barked, "Squad leaders!"

Six aliens stepped over to Jutkelon, though each gave Lan a respectful nod.

Someday, Lan decided, he would have his own army. He liked having the luxuries of life—who wouldn't?—but there was something especially satisfying about having heavily-armed soldiers standing ready to take your orders.

"Kalach, your squad will take this street." Jutkelon drew a faint line down the street that anchored the main gate. "If there's an attack, collect at the gates before advancing. Gressa and Nuez, your squads will concentrate here. It's your task to keep anyone from getting up the hill to the overseer's hut. Dodav and Ghal'z, your teams will be here and here. Your task is to assess whether you're needed at the mine or in the central square. If it's going to be both, Ghal'z will take his soldiers to the square, and Dodav's will go to the mine. Araviha, you station your soldiers in the square, itself. You'll be working with the guards who are already there. I'll tell the guard captain that." He looked at Lan. "Is Heddoran still in charge?"

Lan nodded, but then hesitated slightly. He couldn't remember the guard captain changing, but then this was the sort of thing Gar usually handled.

Damn that male and his betrayal.

Jutkelon saw the flicker in his face. "Do you have concerns about the guards who are already there?"

Lan considered that.

"Before this morning I would have said no," he stated finally. "But my vice-overseer has apparently been working against me, and a strange alien came to see us—someone the guard captain obviously respects, even though he might be a threat."

"Very well." Jutkelon narrowed his eyes as he thought. "Ghal'z, have your squad join Araviha's in the city square, then. I'll have more soldiers on alert to fly in immediately if we need them. Everyone—if you face armed resistance from the guards…" He looked at Lan to determine how he would finish that sentence.

"Kill them," Lan said flatly.

"Kill them," Jutkelon echoed.

To Lan's relief, the soldiers nodded at once. It didn't seem to bother them at all to be taking on their fellow guards from Jutkelon's company. Then again, Lan supposed that facing down someone you knew must be a common occurrence for a mercenary.

"If you have no other questions," he told Jutkelon, "they can set out at once."

"Of course. I have recommendations for the number of provisions to buy, and for a food merchant in Tethra who keeps her mouth shut." Jutkelon handed over a piece of paper.

"Excellent." Lan smiled and walked to his private hopper. "I'll meet you all back at the town."

Aebura was wiping down the bar when a thought flashed into her mind: *soldiers massing by the west road, heading into the mountains. Going to the mines, maybe?*

Oh, no. Oh, no, no, no. Barnabas had to be told.

But how to reach him? She sent out the information as loudly as she could to any Ubuara nearby.

Find me the human named Barnabas, or if you can't, find me

Carter Eastbourne. He's lodging with Diviak down near the gambling halls. She had told the others that the Ranger was going to help the Ubuara still enslaved, and the whole network had been alert for two days.

Barnabas had to know what he was walking into. Aebura had no doubts at all that those soldiers worked for Venfaldri Lan. He was going to act soon. She paced, her tail lashing back and forth. What to do, what to do?

A thought occurred to her. When Barnabas had come here, he'd said he was going to free the mine soon. Perhaps this wasn't Lan's response to that, but rather Barnabas had learned about the soldiers before they had left and was *already* fixing things?

It was possible. It really was.

Her tail lashed again. Yes, it was possible—but she still had to do what she could to make *sure* Barnabas was prepared.

She sent another message. *Anyone who can get into the mountains, go now. The human Barnabas can hear mind-speech, so be* loud. *Tell him that there are soldiers going to Lan's mine. Make sure he knows what to expect.*

It wasn't long before a thought came back from a young Ubuara she knew named Oemuga. She recognized his thoughts because they always made her want to sneeze, like fresh-cracked spicy herbs. *I have a hopper. I will take it and go. I will make sure he finds out.*

Be safe, Aebura told him anxiously. *Please, be safe.*

What is it worth to be safe, he asked her, *if part of us dies? We have to try to save them all.*

16

Following Leiguba's instructions, Gar had snuck out the back of the second jail hut and secreted himself under the general store. With the ground sloping so sharply, most buildings had stilts on one side so that the floors could be level—or at least close to level—and there was plenty of space for most types of aliens.

Also spiders. And rodents.

When he saw those, Gar seriously considered going back to the jail cell. He hated any type of insect. He always had. Someone had brought spiders to Luvendi aboard a ship, and they'd spread through the towers with unnatural speed, skittering up walls and...

Still, he knew he was never going to get an opportunity like this again. He meditated briefly and curled his long form into the shadows.

He had to wait until dark to sneak off toward the mines. While the guards sometimes had trouble telling the faces of the workers apart, Gar had one of the most recognizable faces in the town. He couldn't even disguise himself as another Luvendi—he and Lan were the only two here.

The sun was already sinking, but it was a very long couple of hours before a Nekubi slithered under the floorboards with him.

Gar recognized him and sighed internally—Chogaru, a notorious troublemaker. Gar might be sorry for some of the things he'd done under Lan's orders, but after spending months cleaning up Chogaru's messes and trying to diffuse the situation every time he started a riot, Gar didn't like the Nekubi very much.

Of course this was who Leiguba had sent to him. Chogaru was one of the leaders of the discontented workers. If Gar wanted to get out of this mess he was going to have to work with them, Chogaru included.

He didn't have to be happy about it, though.

"Chogaru." He inclined his head.

"Save it. Leiguba is a fool." Chogaru spat on the ground near Gar's feet. "I came here to tell you the deal's off. There's no way I'd trust you with a scrap of information about the rebellion."

"So why *are* you here, then?" Gar gave him a contemptuous look. "Breaking secrecy and all that."

Chogaru snorted. "It's not exactly a secret that I'm involved. You know about me. You apparently know about Leiguba, too. But those are the only two names you'll get. I'm not going to let you stab us in the back. As far as I'm concerned you can rot under here, or you can go back to your jail cell and take whatever punishment Lan gives you."

Panic rose in Gar's throat. His hearts were beating out of sync, a jarring sensation that made him dizzy.

"No. I can't go back. I don't want to die."

"I really don't care." Chogaru crossed his arms. His thick body was still, his eyes locked on Gar's.

"I will help you! I can't let Lan kill me for—"

"I'm guessing this is going to be a pretty long monologue in which you try to convince me that you're somehow different from him, but I'm not going to listen. You've been carrying out his orders for years. Whatever differences you have now, they aren't important to the rest of us. Powerful people are always having fights—and people like *us* get crushed between them. You want to help? Go back to your cell and let Lan execute you without getting anyone else involved."

"I *can't* go back!"

"Of course you can. You're just a coward."

"Fine, I'm a coward." Gar spat the words. "I don't want to die. You know what I told Leiguba when he came to rescue me? I told him not to trust me. Ask him, if you don't believe me. I told him honestly. I only sided with that human because I was afraid *he'd* kill me. Turns out that only bought me a few days."

"Another lie," Chogaru growled angrily. "The human isn't going to help us. He doesn't care."

Gar began to laugh. He couldn't help himself, though he knew he had to get himself under control before any of the guards heard him.

"That's where you're wrong," he told the Nekubi when he stopped laughing. Chogaru was still there, which was odd, but that realization was quickly gone as Gar thought about Barnabas. "He actually cares when people do unjust things. He *does* care."

"No one cares," Chogaru declared. "Not in the end. It's all pretty words, but when you look at their actions, people only save their own skins. They forget all about anyone else who's being hurt."

"Not this human," Gar argued. "I don't care what you say. Call it just pretty speeches, but he's *going* to free this place."

"You have evidence of that?"

"He asked me for security details: the walls, the guards, all of that sort of stuff. He sent me looking for how Lan is going to get off-planet when he finally leaves. Do you even know what Lan did?"

Chogaru stilled. "No."

"The mines were all shut down." Gar leaned forward and spoke softly and venomously. "I found out about it when I was in Tethra last time. The company was bought out. They released all our contracts immediately and told the overseers the mines were supposed to close. All of them did it...except Lan's. That's why we've had all the new orders. He doesn't answer to the company anymore."

Chogaru looked furious for a moment, then a change came over him. He looked grim—and determined.

"I see," he replied softly. "Very interesting."

Gar waited with his arms crossed over his chest. When the Nekubi said nothing Gar added persuasively, "I have *already* worked against Lan. He had me thrown in jail because I told him I wanted a bigger share of the profits—"

"Oh, and you really didn't?" Chogaru asked acidly.

Gar lifted a shoulder. In a strange way, he liked Chogaru. Other revolutionaries were so *earnest*. It was hard to connect with them. They were like Leiguba, full of bleeding-heart sentiment; too quick to trust, too ready to stake everything on plans that had a big chance of hurting them in the end.

Chogaru was different. He had already told Gar he was only fighting for his own skin, and that he didn't trust anyone else to care. That sort of pragmatism appealed to Gar. He could understand it.

"I've always been ambitious," Gar told him honestly. "And now my ambition is to live. If that means helping the rebellion, I have no problem doing so." He did not add, *And if it means helping Lan I'll do that, too.*

Chogaru considered his words.

"I told Leiguba that he should move tonight," Gar said. "The human is gone and I don't know when he's coming back, but when Lan gets paranoid he wants to kill everyone. I've only *barely* managed to keep him from doing so before, and I'm not with him now. I've told Leiguba everything I know, and he'll be starting the plan an hour after nightfall. You don't have to involve me any further if you don't want to, but just remember that I helped you."

"I will," Chogaru said. "But I'll also remember everything else you've done. I haven't decided yet what I want to do about it."

He slithered out without another word, leaving Gar still huddled under the floor. It had grown darker while they talked; nightfall was no more than a few minutes away.

Leiguba would be putting the plan into action soon if he were wise.

Once out in the open air, Chogaru came to a decision. Lan had never been more vulnerable, and Chogaru had never been more useful. Unlike Gar, he wasn't going to be so stupid as to demand a higher payment up front. No, he'd learn Lan's operation, skim what he could from the profits, and take over at an advantageous moment.

He slithered along in the shadow of one of the walls until he came to a lone guard.

"I need to speak to Lan. There's a rebellion brewing, and he should know about it."

"*You* want to speak to Lan." The guard shook his massive head at him. "I know who you are. I'm not stupid."

"I'm his informant…did you know *that*?" Chogaru smiled coldly at the look of surprise on the guard's face. "Don't take my word for it, though. Tell him I'm requesting to speak with him and see what he says."

He waited while the guard radioed the hut, then held out his hands for cuffs to complete the little show they put on for the other workers.

Soon he wouldn't have to do this anymore.

In the hut, Lan looked at him coldly. "I assume this is important."

"Gar has escaped and there's a rebellion set to start tonight," Chogaru said without preamble. Every once in a while it was good to shock people—and he was pleased to see Lan go still.

But the Luvendi wasn't scared, not entirely. Instead, Lan smiled.

"How long do we have?"

"An hour maybe, but probably less."

"Hmm." Lan typed out a brief message on a communications tablet. "Well, then, thank you for the warning. It will be taken care of."

"By crushing it once it starts?" Chogaru asked shrewdly.

"I don't have to explain my plans to you."

"You don't, but you also don't understand the mood of the camp." Chogaru waved off the guards—awkwardly, given the cuffs—and glided closer to Lan. "Trust me, it would be *far* better to drag them out of their beds and make an example of them than it will be to kill them once they start rioting."

"Why?"

"Because right now other people know about the rebellion, even if they're not involved. If you demonstrate that you have sources, they'll think twice about getting involved. If you wait until the riots start, on the other hand, there will be innocent bodies in the street. Some of those will be your guards'. Then you might have people joining the rebellion who wouldn't have before. Don't let them martyr themselves in a blaze of glory. Show them you know and see everything."

Lan sat back and considered this. His brows were raised contemplatively.

"Interesting."

Chogaru waited.

"Who broke Gar out of prison, by the way?" Lan asked.

There were many ways to answer this. Which would reap the most benefit?

For months, Chogaru had given vague answers. It was time to prove his worth by being specific. "I checked. It was one of the Ubuara—Leiguba. A long-time member of the rebellion, but one who has always advocated caution until now."

"Leiguba." Lan marked something down and nodded to the two guards. "When we begin, tell the guards to search for him in particular." He looked at Chogaru. "What other names do you have for me?"

Not a leader who could be appeased with just a taste, then. Chogaru didn't hesitate, however. He had to show which side he was on. He named every one of the rebellious workers he could think of, pausing to give identifying characteristics and details about what support they gave.

He was not surprised when Lan ordered, "You will accompany my soldiers tonight and point out members of the rebellion to them."

Chogaru knew Lan hoped he would die in the crossfire. Perhaps he would even give secret orders to that effect. As far as he was concerned, Chogaru had served his purpose.

The Nekubi was not offended. He knew this was nothing more than Lan trying to make the smartest moves.

He didn't intend to die, either. He would be watching his back tonight. He would perform well enough to become Lan's second-in-command, and when the time was right he would take over. It would not be today. He did not think the guards would accept so quick a shift. But if there was time; if they saw him in Gar's place...

No one cared who was overseer here. They simply hated whoever had the job.

In fact, Chogaru would cut the guards in on it when he decided to make his move so he could stave off their hatred for a little while. He would let them know what Lan had done and raise their wages, and tell them to keep the information from the workers.

Guilt and greed would do the rest.

He had to be careful not to smile. He nodded to Lan to show he understood his orders. "I know where each of them sleeps. I will be able to assist. You should consider sending guards to the mine entrance and to ring the walls. It is probable that people will try to run and hide."

He was careful not to give orders—not yet. Lan had to see the value of his suggestions first, and become accustomed to taking them. Chogaru made a mental note to have guards around as often as possible when he did this. Then, when he took over, the whispers would say, "He was always the one making the decisions anyway."

Appearances were important.

"Take him to the first jail hut," Lan instructed. "There will be a call for me from the gates very soon. Patch me through immediately and wait for my signal. I'll tell you when to begin and who to arrest."

When they were gone, Lan went to one of his hidden cabinets and withdrew a bottle of *uzi*, a Luvendi liqueur that even most Luvendi did not like. It was native to his tower in particular and it tasted of salt and the sea, having both a harsh burn on the tongue and a flavor as deep as the black water outside the lowest levels. He drank it when he was homesick.

Why he was homesick now he could not have said. But he sipped the drink slowly as he watched the clock above the door, and when the buzzer rang to indicate an incoming call he drained the glass and stood.

It was time. When he thought about what was going to happen, he felt a flutter of excitement. They had been wondering for months what he could really *do* to them if they rebelled. He knew they had.

Tonight he would answer the question.

17

In the cave above the camp, Barnabas slid a light vambrace onto his forearm and flexed his hand as it settled into place. He could have armor that suited any aesthetic, so Barnabas chose to have armor that reminded him of his faith.

When he had mentioned this, others had asked him if he intended to have religious symbols on it and suggested a silver or gold finish.

Barnabas had only smiled.

His armor was an unadorned brown, already beginning to look battered around the edges. For all the world it looked like plain leather armor, though of course it would protect him against far more. The alloys and plastics they used allowed for any part of his armor to dissipate kinetic energy with remarkable ease. A bullet at close range might alter his path, but it would not punch a hole in him. It wouldn't even bruise very much.

Although pain really was an excellent teacher, Barnabas preferred to confine those lessons to the sparring mats.

Gauntlets slid on after the vambraces, then cuisses and greaves, followed by incredibly light pauldrons. Barnabas had been informed that armor components had new names now, but he had not taken the time to learn them.

Armor still had a ritualistic significance to him. Preparing for battle was a contemplative time. He went over his reasons and examined his methods. He was ready to kill without hesitation and he knew plans could change in an instant, but he liked to assure himself that his plan that would lead to the least bloodshed.

The workers are all inside the huts, Shinigami reported. *We're coming up on a shift change, but the soldiers you heard about are almost at the gates. If you want to strike before they get there—*

I don't. I want to strike right when they get through the gates.

Oh?

I want to send a message to the mercenaries of this planet as well. Protection and defense of the helpless are worthy goals, but when the mercenaries help enforce slavery, Bethany Anne will hold them responsible. Being mercenaries does not absolve them of their moral responsibilities.

You know what this would be a great time for, don't you? Missile strikes.

Actually, you have a point.

So, can I?

Maybe. Which do you *think would be more impressive—a missile strike, or a whole company of soldiers cut down by one person?*

Dammit. I wanted to use the missiles.

I appreciate your honesty, and I feel confident that it's going to happen at some point. Be patient.

Shinigami grumbled but comforted herself by hacking the security camera feeds. Barnabas had a point. Lots of people had missiles. Not many people could tear people limb from limb.

And hell if she was going to miss watching *that*.

Leiguba had acted as normally as he could in the hours before bed. He'd made the commotion to distract the guards at the jail hut, but he'd been able to get away before they caught him.

Normally he wouldn't have chanced that, because the Brakalons generally couldn't tell the different Ubuara apart so they would report the incident to Lan without giving any names. Lan would then order all of the Ubuara punished the next day.

But if this worked, by tomorrow Lan wouldn't have the chance to hurt them anymore. His tail twitched contentedly.

The members of the rebellion were careful not to look at one another as they went into the huts to sleep. The guards must sense nothing amiss. Anyway, all of them knew the plan. They did not need secret signals or nods.

Leiguba lay in the dark and tried to pretend he was asleep while he counted every second until they started. The Ubuara would undertake the first part of the plan, scaling the walls and racing to the overseer's hut to take Lan captive.

Hopefully the guards would stand down when they did that, but if not the rest of the plan would be put in motion.

Leiguba stared out the window at the stars; only a few minutes now. He'd planned his route in his head, as had the rest of the Ubuara. They would each go different ways so that if one of them was caught the others could just keep going.

He flexed his hands, then clenched them. He must go as fast as he could. He—

The door burst open and his hutmates started screaming. Bright lights pierced the darkness, blinding the people inside, and guards peered about suspiciously as they waded into the pile of Ubuara. With them was Chogaru, who pointed directly at Leiguba.

"Him." He looked around and effortlessly identified the rest of the Ubuara. "There. There. That one's getting out the window—catch him! And there. Those are the ones you want from here."

"Chogaru!" Leiguba did not struggle as the guards picked him up and secured his arms. He knew he was not strong enough to fight them, so instead he focused his attention on the Nekubi. "Chogaru, what did they threaten you with?"

"Nothing." Chogaru smiled. "From the first day I came here, I have reported on all of you."

"What?" It was like being punched in the stomach—or perhaps one of the guards actually had. Leiguba struggled to breathe.

"You wanted to rebel, but that's not going to work." The Nekubi shrugged. "People like Lan have the power, Leiguba. You have to get a bit of it for yourself, not try to fight it head-on." He looked at the guards. "Come on. I'll show you the rest in the other huts."

"*Chogaru!*" But he was gone, and the guards dragged Leiguba and his fellow conspirators into the night.

———

When the first screams came to him on the wind, Lan crossed his arms and smiled. The guards had moved quickly.

He hadn't let the new soldiers in yet. When Jutkelon had asked him whether he trusted them Lan had realized the danger at once. Just as Gar had betrayed Lan, the guards might betray him.

He was coping with the one betrayal, but he had to be open to the possibility of another. Thus, he was giving the guards below a chance to prove themselves before he intervened. If they did not, he had his new soldiers.

In the meantime, he would stand and watch as the operation unfolded. He was *savoring* it.

You want to defy me? His lip curled. *It will cost you more than you could have imagined.*

———

It was really remarkable, Chogaru thought dispassionately. Technology had advanced so far and so fast. There were lights one could put in living quarters that took almost no energy to run and would last several lifetimes. There were building materials and structures that could resist nearly anything.

Yet most of the people of the universe lived in squalid little huts like these. The best technologies did not get sent to these places. Instead of well-built huts that would last for generations, overseers invariably used the same old materials to build poorly-constructed rat-traps that were always in need of repair.

And on nights like these, with people screaming in the darkness and the guards holding torches. Actual flaming torches, of all the stupid things?

You could really see how shoddy it all was.

He looked around at the screaming people and the dirt and the flames and felt nothing but contempt for all of it. He was all for patient progress, but when this was over he was done with this place and would never look back.

Lan really was stupid, if he was content to make this his best cash-grab rather than using it to go for more.

One of the families waited until the coast was clear and then snuck out of a house and headed up the hill toward the mine. Chogaru shouted for the guards and pointed.

"Are they rebels?" one of them asked him. He did not call Chogaru "sir."

Chogaru memorized his face. "No," he said icily, "but they are trying to escape. Make sure they stay here in case it turns out they *have* been complicit."

The guard went over doubtfully. First he tried to usher the family back down the hill, waving his hands as he explained. He wasn't acting very strong, Chogaru noted. If he were that family, he would think this guard didn't really want to follow Lan's orders.

But when the parents made a break for it, pulling their child along with them, the guard did what he had to do. He grabbed the child and dragged it back toward the camp, knowing the parents would follow.

Chogaru nodded when the guard returned, pointedly ignoring his miserable expression. In the flickering light he realized it was not just any guard, but Heddoran, the captain.

He of all people should know better. Chogaru would remember this.

He had the sense of being watched and turned his head. There, through the jail's front window: Leiguba. Chogaru turned away coldly. Leiguba needed to remember that this wasn't personal. The Ubuara had done stupid things and Chogaru had not, so Chogaru was out here directing things and Leiguba was in jail.

There was no reason for Leiguba to be staring at him as if this had been some sort of betrayal. Chogaru had stepped in to fill a gap in the system of this town. It was natural.

In the jail cell, Leiguba slumped against the wall. Chogaru. It was *Chogaru* they shouldn't have trusted.

How could he have known? And what the hell did they do *now*?

"Keep *moving*." Gar hissed. He beckoned to the children and pointed under the general store, shoving them underneath roughly when they cried about how dark it was. "*Quiet!* You want the guards to hear you?" The children's protests subsided and Gar pointed to one of the oldest.

"You…keep the rest of them quiet, and make sure no one goes running off. I'm going to get help."

The child nodded jerkily, and Gar looked around before slipping off. He watched Chogaru and the guards for a moment, then headed up the hill towards the mine—and the cave.

This was the stupidest thing he'd ever done. He'd still been under the porch and had been paralyzed by indecision when everything began. He should have taken advantage of the chaos and leave all of this behind or, failing that, he should just have stayed under there and hoped that no one noticed him.

Instead, he'd grabbed children as they and their parents ran past in terror and hid them, and now he was going to fetch Barnabas.

This was going to get him killed. Why, after a lifetime of doing the smart thing, was he not doing so when it counted the most?

Barnabas had just sunk down on a rock to go over the plan in his head once more when the screams began.

Shinigami, what's happening? He didn't dare risk sound until he knew what was happening.

Something is going on in the town. Guards are going into the huts and taking people out, and the soldiers are just waiting outside the gates.

Where are the guards taking people?

Into the jails.

And Lan?

Watching it all. One second...zooming in. He looks smug, the sonofabitch.

Barnabas swore under his breath.

I caught some of that. How do you fuck a moose sideways?

Barnabas slanted a look upward and forbore to answer.

Fine, don't tell me. I'll just look on the datanet... OH GOD, NEVER SEARCH FOR THAT.

Barnabas palmed his face. *I could have warned you. Why would you think it was a good idea?*

I thought it was figurative!

That's how I meant it, certainly, but... Look, we don't have time for this right now. What the fuck is Lan playing at?

I don't know, but the other one is coming for you. Reviewing the security tapes, it looks like he hid some of the children.

Barnabas didn't wait for Gar to reach him; he yanked the Luvendi into the cave. "What's going on?"

"Oh, thank everything—you're here!" Gar tried to peel Barnabas' fingers off his shirt but gave up fairly quickly. His strength would have been no match for the *kalanon*, much less the Ranger when he was angry. "Where have you *been*? Lan has gone off the deep end! There was a rebellion set to go tonight because they were afraid that if you didn't get back in time they'd all be killed."

Barnabas swore, this time more inventively and in Latin. He should have been there. He should have headed this off.

You know what time it is, right?

I do. He let go of Gar's shirt and went to arm himself. *It's time to make them very,* very *sorry they pulled this shit.*

Finally.

"Gar? If you wanted to get the guards to stand down, what would you do?"

"I'd start with Heddoran. He was very impressed that you were a religious man."

"Very well. Go speak to him." Barnabas waved him off. "Feel free to start with religion, and move on to self-interest if that doesn't work. It's like this, you see." He smiled coldly. "Whoever is still defending Lan and carrying out his orders when I get to them dies."

18

"Stop! Everybody stop!" His voice was carried away by the wind as Gar ran down the hill waving his arms. "*STOP!*"

On the opposite side of the small valley, Lan frowned. There was no mistaking that tall thin figure, and it had come out of the cave Chogaru had mentioned earlier. So Gar *had* been working with Barnabas.

His death would not only be public, it would be *painful* as well.

Shinigami tried to capture his voice to blast it from the loudspeakers, but couldn't. Too much interference, she supposed. She said as much to Barnabas.

He's on his own, Barnabas told her grimly. *I'm giving him a two-minute head start, and that's only good as long as they don't hurt anyone.*

Gar, having picked up considerable speed on the slope, burst into the center of the town. "Stop," he blurted. He bent over to catch his breath, bracing his hands on his knees, and held up a hand for silence.

"He was arrested earlier," Chogaru told the guards coldly. "Bring him back to his cell."

"Wait!" Gar forced himself to stand and held his hands out beseechingly. "Just wait. *Please*. A moment. I bring a message from...from..." He looked at Heddoran. "From the *kalanon*. He takes exception to all this. He says it is slavery, and he is obliged to intervene. He would have you stand aside so these people can be freed."

Chogaru gave a snort. "Do you hear yourself? This is ridiculous."

Gar presently had nothing to lose, just as when he had stared down Barnabas in the room in Tethra, and now, as then, Gar felt a strange calm come over him. He met Heddoran's eyes.

"I think you know that what you are doing is not right, Heddoran. I see it in your expression. You do not like chasing down children and hauling their parents away screaming in the dead of night."

"This is *ridiculous*." Chogaru's voice had risen. "Take him back to his cell or kill him, but be done with it."

"Shut up." Heddoran swung his head to look briefly at Chogaru.

"*What?*"

"*Shut. Up*. I don't like you." Heddoran looked up the hill to Lan's hut. "And I have not liked the overseer's orders for some time. But I *do* like the *kalanon*."

"He is a..." Gar struggled to find words. How did one describe what he had seen? "He is a warrior," he explained diplomatically. "He could triumph over all of you, but he has chosen—out of respect for you, Heddoran—to give you the chance to stand down."

There was a pause. Chogaru looked between the two of them and the guards looked uncertainly at Heddoran. Everyone had frozen when Gar arrived. Some of the guards had been dragging workers, and the workers were still as well—too enthralled by the scene to pull away from the guards.

Gar forced himself not to look around, but he was very aware of the guards at his back—and of the heavy pistols they had not yet used tonight.

"Stand down," Heddoran commanded.

Gar sagged with relief, and he could have sworn he felt the same emotion ripple through the guards. Workers were helped to their feet and cuffs were undone.

"Don't listen to him," Chogaru shouted. "You work for Venfaldri Lan, overseer of this mine. You could be hauled up in front of a court for dereliction of duty! You were hired for *security*, not for—"

Heddoran stomped over to Chogaru and bent down so his heavy head was nose to nose with the Nekubi, who broke off with a strangled gasp.

"I told you to shut up," Heddoran growled. "You speak of my contract? What of these people? Everyone knows they should have left months ago."

There was a murmur of assent from the workers.

"We should put *you* in the jail," Heddoran stated simply. He looked up at the hill. "Along with Lan." He looked down at his radio, which was still transmitting, and smiled. "Did you hear that, Lan?"

Lan had heard the whole thing as it happened. He gave a terse command, and everyone in the valley heard the screech of the gates opening.

Go for Lan. Don't let him get away.

Barnabas cast a look at the Luvendi and shook his head. *No. It's going to be a massacre if I don't go now.* He paused and smiled. *Well, it's going to be a massacre if I do go.*

With that, he took three steps and launched himself from the hillside.

His footwear might look like well-worn leather boots, but they were far more than that. His jump carried him over the town square and he landed in a cloud of dust in front of the gates as the soldiers began to stream in.

"State your business here." His eyes began to glow red.

"You know our business here." Gressa had been a mercenary long enough to know the rhythm of a fight—and when to disrupt it. "You should—" Still speaking, he casually flipped his gun up and fired point-blank at Barnabas's head.

Barnabas still stood. The bullet had flattened itself against his gauntlet, since he had thrown his hand up in front of his face as soon as he's seen Gressa's fingers twitch toward his gun.

How did you know he meant to shoot you in the head?

He's a seasoned mercenary. He's not going to shoot me in the chest and have me live long enough to shoot him back.

Barnabas looked at all of them. Their mouths were hanging open. They had never seen anyone move so fast.

But they were well trained, so a moment later they raised their weapons. To their surprise, when Barnabas next spoke he had very long, *very* sharp fangs.

"Wrong. Answer."

Gressa didn't even hear the words. His head had been

severed from his body and was bouncing on the ground by the time Barnabas had finished speaking.

Gressa wasn't the only one who knew the rhythms of a fight. Barnabas recognized the absolute shock that froze the mercenaries, and he knew it would wear off in a moment.

He would win even if he let them recover, of course, but he still had Lan to deal with once he was done with them.

Shinigami, he said, his mental tone even and calm as he unholstered his Jean Dukes Specials and took out two of the other squad leaders. *Do me a favor.*

Yes? Shinigami peered through his eyes as the soldiers flowed around him. They weren't shooting, since they had been foolish enough to surround him entirely. They knew they would catch one another in the crossfire.

It would have been smart to stay where they were and fire in waves.

But they weren't *being* smart. He had gotten under their skin when he'd killed Gressa and they were now reduced to primal instinct, aware on some deep level that they were going to die.

If you see Lan escaping, Barnabas told her, *let him go unless it's into a shuttle that can take him off-planet. Just track him.*

You said I was going to get to use missiles.

And you will. One moment.

Barnabas could identify three more leaders from their original formation. He picked one off with a single shot and leapt clear over the crowd to land behind another. His impossibly-sharp knife easily pierced the creature's torso.

The squad leader screamed, but he didn't seem to be bleeding very much.

His heart is down near his right hip.

Thank you, Shinigami.

Another thrust, and this time purple blood fountained from the wound when Barnabas removed the blade.

Much better, but now I'll have to wash everything.

You know how you could have avoided that, right?

Yes.

Several of the soldiers had finally roused enough to fire on him. Barnabas ducked, bared his teeth, and leapt into the fray once more.

He was laughing like a maniac now. He moved in a blur, pushing himself to the limits of his abilities. Teeth sank into flesh and his knives were coated in blood of varying colors.

Soldiers threw themselves at him, aware only that this was violence and combat and they were trained to deal with that in only one way.

Unfortunately for them, it was the *wrong* way.

They piled on him one after the other but Barnabas always emerged, sending the soldiers staggering away from him as he shot them with their own guns.

"Justice," he whispered as one of them fell to the dirt with a choking gasp. "You chose to be here and to stay. You will pay the price."

"You're a monster!" One of the remaining mercenaries stumbled to his feet, a rifle clutched in trembling hands. "A mutant."

"You have no idea how right you are," Barnabas told

him and nodded at the gun. "Are you going to shoot me or walk away?"

Back in the town square, Gar struggled to breathe as he observed the confrontation.

He had seen Barnabas with his eyes glowing red before, and he supposed he'd believed Barnabas would be able to clear the entire camp.

But *watching* it happen was something else.

The human was beyond scary—a nightmarish beast, all the more terrifying for holding his monstrous impulses in check. His calm and quiet demeanor hadn't fooled Gar, not exactly.

One of the children whimpered and hid its face in Gar's robes, and despite his general dislike of children, he found himself patting it on the shoulder and trying to put himself between it and...that *thing*.

He exchanged a look with the guard captain. *Glad you stood down, aren't you?*

Heddoran just stared at Barnabas, his expression somewhere between fear and reverence.

The mercenary, meanwhile, unleashed an entire magazine at Barnabas. He fired until the barrel started to melt, and he was still firing when Barnabas walked through the stream of bullets to pluck the rifle out of his hands.

Barnabas's fingers came around the mercenary's throat like a vise.

"What. *Are*. You?" the soldier choked out.

"Does it matter?" Barnabas asked him. *I am killing this*

one, right? This isn't another his-heart-is-in-his-hip scenario, is it?

If you mean, are you successfully strangling him, the answer is yes. If you mean, are you killing him in the coolest possible way, the answer would be no because—

Missile strikes. I know.

I was going *to say that thing about pulling someone's spine out and strangling them with it.*

Oh. I suppose I could do that.

You're not going to, though, are you?

No. Barnabas tightened his fingers abruptly and dropped the suddenly-limp body. *Too messy. Don't want to clean my armor.*

Too late!

Barnabas was still laughing as he raised his gun and fired seven perfect shots, felling the remaining mercenaries.

Up on the hill, Lan nearly screamed when a hand grabbed his arm.

"Come on," Jutkelon said tersely.

"Where did you come from?"

"I landed while that massacre was going on. Let's go. I'm getting you out of here." He dragged Lan towards one of the hoppers.

"You came to save me?"

"Call it insurance," Jutkelon replied grimly. "You just cost me nearly a hundred mercenaries. You're going to pay for that, and you're going to help me find out what that thing is so this doesn't happen again."

"He's a human," Lan explained numbly as he strapped himself in. "I can't believe it. He really *was* a human."

"A *human*? Like the Empress?" Jutkelon slammed his hands down on the controls. "And you didn't think to *warn* me about that?"

"Drive! For the love of everything, get out of here!" Lan sank his head into his hands. "I thought it was a joke. I thought they weren't real. His eyes weren't glowing when I met him."

"Look on the bright side," Jutkelon said grimly as the hopper soared into the air.

"What's the bright side?" Lan picked his head up to look.

"Where there are humans, there's Coke."

"What's Coke?"

"You'll see."

Barnabas approached the main square at a leisurely walk. He was aware of guards and workers falling out of his way, white-faced and silent with fear.

Shinigami, any way to do a reverse Fear?

Afraid not. You're covered in blood and they're not going to un-see what you just did. But, sure, go ahead. Try if you want to.

Barnabas sighed.

The guards scattered from the center of the square, leaving a single Nekubi gaping at him.

"Who is this one?" Barnabas asked. He looked around.

"Chogaru, *kalanon*." The guard captain spoke respectfully.

"I see. Thank you. Chogaru, why are these people staring at you like this?"

Chogaru said nothing. He could not speak for fear. This human had just slaughtered all of Lan's soldiers, and there was no running from him. They had all seen that leap. The human should be a bloody smear on the ground, and instead, he was covered in other people's blood.

He was going to have to talk his way out of this.

"I am an information broker, sir." He smiled. "I do what I must to survive. Surely you understand."

"I have survived more," Barnabas said softly, "than you will ever know. To become what I am, I endured horrors and temptations you could not imagine. Let me guess. You sold these people out for some scraps Lan was going to throw you."

Lan is getting away, by the way. Just in a hopper so far. If he gets in a shuttle—

Yes, you can use missiles.

Whoop!

All right, that's definitely *Tabitha's influence.*

"For scraps? No! To save myself. He knew about the rebellion." Chogaru shook his head regretfully. "Surely you know how he kept us—"

"I know that neither the guards nor the rebellion are speaking up for you. Leiguba?" Barnabas looked around.

Leiguba chittered at him from the window of the jail.

"Hello. Leiguba, is what this Nekubi says true?" He already knew it wasn't, of course. He had read Chogaru's mind as he came up to him.

Leiguba shook his head.

"Ah." Barnabas pulled out his gun. *Shinigami, where do I shoot this one?*

In the head.

Thank you.

There was the trademark blast of a Jean Dukes Special and Chogaru slumped dead on the dirt.

Barnabas looked at Heddoran. "The first thing you will do is turn off the mind-speech blocker. Then you and your guards will build new huts for these workers and allow them to take control of the food supplies until I return. You stood down when I asked, but you also participated in these atrocities. Do you deny it?"

"No, *kalanon.*"

Barnabas nodded, satisfied with the answer since he had read the truth in the Brakalon's mind. "I will deal with that when I return. Leiguba, appoint someone to be in charge here and come with me. We're going to Tethra to find Lan and end this."

19

*A*nything happening?

    I told you I would let you know when there was some-thing to report, Shinigami snarked.

Barnabas sighed and rubbed his forehead. *I apologize. I'm...impatient.*

You don't say! And I can't believe I'm the one having to tell you to be patient about a missile strike.

Yes, it's funny how times have changed, isn't it?

Go stretch your legs, Shinigami suggested. *Maybe you'll feel better.*

Barnabas took her advice with another long sigh.

There wasn't much else to do, after all. By the time Leiguba had set everything in order in the mining town, and Barnabas was sure the guards were going to act in good faith and all medical needs had been taken care of, Jutkelon's hopper had set down at his estate on the outskirts of Tethra.

According to Shinigami's report, however, "estate" wasn't exactly the right word. It was more like a fortress.

The walls were a high-grade composite that was resistant to explosives, much of the living space was in underground bunkers, and there were stockpiles of both fuel and food.

There was also the small matter of the three hundred mercenaries who presently lived at the complex.

After scanning the compound, Shinigami concluded that bombing it wouldn't do much good.

If you're *saying that, it must be true.*

Trust me, I'm as disappointed with the situation as you are.

Barnabas was left to stew while Shinigami ran a structural analysis from any and all blueprints and technical readouts she could find, as well as decrypting and analyzing outbound communications. There just wasn't much for him to do.

He didn't like that. Back before AIs, *he* would have been solely responsible for the research and analysis for a project. He liked to say that people who did their own research were better prepared, but his research could never surpass Shinigami's. He *wasn't* the best person for this job, and he shouldn't be upset because the outcome would undoubtedly be better.

He chose to be grumpy anyway—for that reason, and for others he was not particularly keen to think about just yet.

Meanwhile, there was a great deal of work to be done in the town. Barnabas headed down the hill from Lan's hut and found Heddoran explaining the gate mechanisms to a small group of workers.

Barnabas was pleased to see that Heddoran was upholding his part of the bargain about putting the workers in charge and making the mining town a nicer place to live, and the guards took Heddoran's orders without complaint. He paused now to listen to the guard captain's instructions.

"Gar can give you more information about how to control this from the overseer's hut," Heddoran was saying. "From inside the camp, you have to go to the guard barracks *and* any one of the towers to disable the automatic locking mechanism. Even when the system loses power those overrides will keep running because they have batteries, but they need the correct signals to do so. Now, if you're trying to do that without *signals*—"

Barnabas headed onward with a brief nod to the guard captain.

He was still trying to figure out what to do with all the guards and Gar. All had been enormously helpful over the past few hours, but Barnabas was well aware that how they behaved with him watching—and still covered in mercenary blood—was not a good indicator of the long-term.

More than that, there remained the very real problem that while their present and future actions could mitigate the past, they could neither change nor excuse it. Barnabas could kill them, of course. He would hardly break a sweat doing it, either.

But as he had said to Shinigami, he knew what it was to have committed atrocities. He knew what it was to have regrets and to still have value to give the world, even considering his past. It was not arrogance when he said to others that he was one of the best at stopping injustice, ending it *quickly*.

It was a statement of fact.

However, just as with Bethany Anne and the governance of her new territories, he was finding that stopping injustice and booting out old leaders was infinitely less complicated than setting up better systems and dealing with the lesser crimes committed during darker days.

He would ask the workers, he decided. Perhaps they would be vengeful, but perhaps they could suggest something he would not have thought of. He continued to stroll, trying to take in as much as he could of the activity around him without disturbing it.

Nearby, Carter turned his head to watch Barnabas pass.

"Carter Eastbourne, focus!" Aebura gave him a stern look. They were sorting the food from the commissary, all of which had been hauled outside so they could take advantage of the early morning sunlight.

Perhaps everyone should have gone to sleep after Barnabas had ended things late last night, but no one had been able to relax enough for that. As soon as it became clear that Barnabas would not be returning to Tethra at once, Leiguba had summoned Aebura to the town and she had brought many Ubuara with her, as well as Carter.

The human had gone to work with good grace, but he'd been distracted since Barnabas had first come out of the overseer's hut.

"You don't need to say my whole name, you know," he told Aebura.

"I don't want to be rude."

"It's not rude to call me 'Carter,'" he assured her. "And

I'm sorry, I'll get back to work. I just...I've never been this *close* to any of them."

"'Them?'" She labeled a package of some sort of grain, concentrating in order to hold a pen that was made for much larger hands than hers. The Ubuara were unusually small compared to the majority of sentient species in known space.

"The whole team," Carter explained. He hefted the big bag of grain easily and set it with its fellows. "Here, right? There we go. Here's the next one, then." When he'd set that bag near Aebura, he returned to his appointed task of sorting cans by type. "You know, Bethany Anne, the Rangers, the Bitches…"

"'Bitches?' I'm confused. That word seems to have negative connotations in your language."

"It's...a bit more complicated than that. It's a joke." When Aebura frowned, Carter hastened to explain. "The Bitches aren't a joke, it's a joke that they're called… Never mind, this is probably too complicated to explain if English isn't your first language. It's normally an insult, but not for them."

"Carter?"

"Yes?"

"Do humans do *anything* normally?"

Carter started laughing and couldn't stop. He leaned on the table of canned goods and cackled until his eyes were streaming. When he straightened, he had to rub his side because the muscles were cramping.

"Ah," he exclaimed happily. "*This* is what you don't get on the *Meredith Reynolds*. These kinds of questions."

"Bethany Anne gets those kinds of questions," Barnabas observed from directly behind him.

Carter jumped and swore. When he looked around, it was to find a pleasantly smiling Barnabas covered in dried blood. The total effect was, well, *unnerving*.

"Of course," Barnabas continued thoughtfully, "people tend to say it in very diplomatic language, so she's not supposed to laugh. I'd say it was one of the main reasons she disliked those meetings so much."

Carter found that he was opening and closing his mouth like a fish while failing to make any sort of sound at all.

"I'm Barnabas," Barnabas added with a respectful nod.

Yeah, I fucking know. Luckily, Carter's automatic politeness kicked in. "I'm Carter Eastbourne, sir. I'm pleased to meet you."

Barnabas smiled, having heard the unspoken comment, then, "I'd shake your hand," Barnabas said gravely, "but I don't think all the blood is gone."

Carter stared at him, trying to figure out what to say to that.

You're making him uncomfortable, Shinigami told Barnabas.

I know. It's funny.

Well, be nice.

"Be nice?" *Do you have another side to you I haven't seen before?*

I have a sense of propriety, Shinigami said stiffly. *As should you, at* your *age.*

Keep talking like that and you won't *make* it *to this age.*

Barnabas looked around the town. "Mr. Eastbourne, a word?"

Oh, God—the Pepsi. Carter gulped, said a silent prayer, and gave himself up to his fate. "Of course, sir."

"Please, call me Barnabas. Aebura, I'll have him back to you shortly." Barnabas led the way down the main street. When he was a little ways away, he said, "As one of the first humans to immigrate to High Tortuga, I wondered if I might trouble you for some first impressions."

"Yes, of course. Um, on what part specifically?" Carter resisted the urge to wipe his palms on his pants.

"Perhaps you might start by telling me a bit about yourself."

Was this it? Was this the trap? Did he think Carter would be stupid enough to admit his Pepsi affiliation? Carter vowed to be canny. He wouldn't be duped so easily. "Well, I have a wife, sir—Barnabas, sorry—and twins. Alanna and Samuel. I wanted to set up a business here first and then bring them. I've been, ah..." Just in time, he remembered that he shouldn't rat out Aebura.

He was too late. "Working with Aebura," Barnabas said smoothly. "Yes, I know. She mentioned you to me. I think it speaks volumes that when it came time to rebuild this place she asked you to come and help. From what Shinigami has dug up, Ubuara are very protective of the members of their community, so they're cautious about who they allow into their circle."

"Really?" Carter felt a flush of pride.

Barnabas stopped, looking very serious. "She told me that you offered to help her with the mine before you knew I was involved. I wanted to thank you."

"Oh, it was no trouble." Carter felt somehow like a little kid again, totally inadequate in the face of Barnabas's calm presence. He wondered if it was true that Barnabas had been a monk once, or just a prank story spread by...Tabitha, maybe. If the rumors were true, Ranger Two had quite a sense of humor.

Then again, the aura of calm Barnabas had when he looked at Carter made it seem quite likely that he *had* been a monk. Somehow it fit.

"It *would* have been trouble," Barnabas replied, somehow both grave and amused at once, "and you know it. The fact that you offered to help? Well, I know we brought many of Earth's best with us when we came here, but it is always gratifying to see it in action."

Carter flushed.

"They'll need us," Barnabas continued. "You know that. They don't need our businesses or for us to buy from them; that isn't what I mean. Our citizens will be just like anyone else in that respect. What they need from us is to remind them that Bethany Anne looks out for her own, and that her laws are enforced. They need to know that even when I am not here, her laws will be strong because she and her people uphold them in word and deed."

Carter stood a bit taller. "I understand, sir." He caught the title as it came out of his mouth and smiled self-consciously. "I think that's just going to be how I address you. Sorry."

Barnabas smiled.

You like that, Shinigami accused. *You're so old-fashioned.*

I like good manners, and I'm indisputably his elder.

Barnabas started walking again and waited for Carter

to fall in beside him. "Where do you think the trouble will come?"

Carter considered this. "All the usual places, I'd guess. I don't know much about that. But from what I've seen so far, I think there will be a bunch of smaller-grade problems. Friction. You see, the people who came here—they were all running from something. Maybe that's a bad way to say it. They came here to make a life for themselves because they were stifled where they were." He looked at Barnabas. "They're all fiercely independent, and while they might not mind the idea of abolishing *slavery*, you can bet even some people who don't like slavery will get upset about you taking the fight to Jutkelon."

"Ah. You were eavesdropping."

"I...ah...er..."

"No, no, I wasn't being particularly secretive about it, it's all right." Barnabas looked up as Leiguba ran by and nodded to him. "Hello, Leiguba. Have you met Carter?"

Yes. Aebura introduced us. Leiguba nodded at Carter. *She likes you. She says—*

"Carter isn't able to speak mind to mind," Barnabas explained.

Leiguba chittered. "You can't all do that?"

"No. I...have some upgrades."

Carter sighed. He didn't have any fun upgrades. He'd always wanted to try out some of the tech they were working on for the inner circle, even if Elisa had said he was being ridiculous.

Leiguba waved and headed off again, and Carter looked at Barnabas. "In any event, sir, I think what you'll find is that even when people agree with the laws we have, they might not be happy about the idea of being subject to laws at all."

"They'll have to come to terms with it," Barnabas said simply. "Bethany Anne does not impose laws for no reason. She respects individual autonomy. What laws she has are there for good reason."

"I don't disagree, sir. You just asked where we would have problems."

"I think," Barnabas said after a moment, "that perhaps it will even itself out. Those who cannot abide it will leave, and those who like it might settle here." He frowned. "Or not. Part of my mandate is to make sure this planet is as much of a secret as possible. In the meantime…"

"They'll see how you deal with Jutkelon and Lan," Carter told him. "People push back a lot more when they think there's wiggle room. You don't strike me as the type to give any wiggle room at all."

"I wish it were that simple," Barnabas murmured. "But I see your point, yes. The larger infractions—those will be met with no compromise or leniency." He smiled. "Thank you for your help, Mr. Eastbourne. I wish you a great deal of luck with your…what was it Aebura said you were planning? To manufacture Coke? Bethany Anne would be pleased."

He smiled inscrutably and headed off, leaving Carter staring after him with wide eyes.

It was absolutely impossible to know what Barnabas knew and what he did not know.

He was a canny opponent.

20

"I don't understand," Lan snapped. "Why not just bomb the damned thing into oblivion?"

It had been a long night, and he was very tired. Jutkelon had not wanted to rest when they arrived in Tethra. He had wanted to begin planning at once, and now here they were half a day later with Lan aching with tiredness and Jutkelon growing ever angrier.

An angry Brakalon was not what you wanted in any situation.

Indeed, Jutkelon put his fist down on the table in a way that suggested he would rather smash it to bits—and reminded Lan that he could easily do that. Most Brakalons were big, and Jutkelon was bigger even than most of his kind. He could rip doors off hinges. Lan shuddered to think how many bullets it would take to kill the man.

He had always resented how helpless he felt around Brakalons.

"We will not bomb the mine," Jutkelon told him with exaggerated courtesy, "except as a last resort."

Lan stared at him resentfully.

"What do you do when someone challenges you for what is yours?" Jutkelon asked, finally annoyed enough to try asking rather than telling.

"Fight them," Lan replied sulkily.

"Exactly. Fight them. Why are you not doing that?"

"I *am* doing it! I'm suggesting bombing it. Letting everyone else know—"

"What, that you'll always have to be starting over because as soon as someone challenges you, you smash everything like a child?" Jutkelon glared.

"What do *you* care, anyway?"

"He killed a hundred of my soldiers!" Jutkelon slammed both hands on the table. Everything on it jumped, and Lan went rigid with fear. "He thinks he can come in here and tell us what to do and how to behave. I heard that warning Gar gave them. Anyone choosing to defend you would be killed. You cannot show weakness to people like that."

"Which is why I suggested—"

"If you destroy everything you have that someone else wants, you'll be left with nothing at all." Jutkelon stared Lan down. "What you need to do is fight for it. No matter how costly they make it for you, make it worse for them. What they try to take from you, you defend until they walk away, and when they turn their back you kill them. You show everyone watching that what's yours is *yours*."

Lan stared at him. He was at a loss. He didn't understand—and he didn't think Jutkelon had the first idea of what he was doing.

Had he not *seen* what had happened?

"You can't kill that human," he said finally.

"*Anyone* can be killed." Jutkelon's voice was a growl. "You, that human, even his Queen."

Lan had thoughts on the inadvisability of trying to kill the other two on that list, but he kept them to himself. Jutkelon didn't seem to be in a very reasonable mood right now.

"What would you suggest, then?" he asked finally. "If you think he should be fought and one hundred soldiers weren't enough—"

"They weren't enough, but they also weren't deployed correctly. Think about it—he went there to take you down, but when he could easily have done so he did not. Why?"

Lan shrugged.

Jutkelon rolled his eyes, "Because he was trying to protect the workers, you fool. He cares more about their safety than capturing you. If we hold the workers hostage, the cost of freeing the mine will be too great. *He* will know he can take it from you only by destroying it, rather than the opposite."

Lan considered this. "But he was able to do it last time."

"Because Heddoran listened to him," Jutkelon grumbled. "To think I trained that son of a *laldar koresht.* He's gone soft."

Lan shrugged. He really didn't care about Jutkelon's take on the situation.

"Show strength and keep the right people around you, and nothing like that will happen again," Jutkelon told him. "And we don't have to resort to burning it all down just yet, but we *do* need something that will make an impression. So I've called in help."

"I assume you're planning to bill me for it."

"In part." Jutkelon smiled. "After all, it's your mess. If you'd just killed the human when he arrived, we wouldn't be dealing with this issue. But I understand that this threat is not just to you, so I will not make you responsible for the whole cost. You were only ever meant to be an example. We will make the human the example instead."

"*How?* You keep giving speeches, but nothing gets done." When Jutkelon glared, Lan swallowed. "I'm sorry."

"You will be if you don't stop whining." Jutkelon shrugged. "I called in some ships. Let's just say, the number of mercenaries this human *thinks* he's dealing with is nowhere close to the number I have called in. He thinks we're weak. He thinks we're stupid, that we only run headlong into battle. He'll learn how wrong he is. People who think they're clever are easy to manipulate."

Lan gave a hesitant nod.

He hoped Jutkelon's confidence was justified.

Barnabas sipped at his fruit juice and tried to relax. The tangy sweetness slid across his tongue, a flavor he would liken to…

Shinigami, tell me about this fruit.

It's called hakoj.

You already did an analysis on the beverage? That was fast.

I'd love to take credit for that, but what I actually did was look at the fruit pallets in the alley behind the bar.

Barnabas gave a small smile. *Okay, so tell me about* hakoj. *Ubuara fruit, yes?*

Yes. Native to planet Dugan. While we're on the topic—did

you know Luvendan might not actually be the Luvendi home planet?

The names don't leave much to the imagination.

Don't be so short-sighted. It could simply be that the ones who emigrated there called themselves that.

I hadn't thought of that. He drained his glass and smiled as Aebura swung over with a fresh glass. "Thank you. You must have been watching for when I finished the glass."

She only smiled in response. Out loud, at least. *Can you hear me?*

Barnabas frowned. He had heard something and guessed from her intent expression that she was trying to communicate, but her thoughts were whisper-soft, like a murmur in another language.

Apparently it was easier for him to get the sense of an Ubuara being present and send his thoughts to them than it was for them to hear him.

How clearly can you hear me? He made no special effort to send the thought.

Aebura frowned in concentration and Barnabas sighed. "It seems we have to make quite an effort to hear each other's thoughts."

"Oh." Aebura nodded thoughtfully. "Well, that is good to know." She leapt to the rafters and swung away.

I wonder why she tried that.

They're curious, Shinigami told him. *Even I can tell you that. You show up out of nowhere, help them free their friends, and you can speak mind to mind. That's rare among alien species.*

Mmm. Tell me about Luvendan.

Well, there's no stable landmass on the planet, and no records

197

of ice ages or anything else that would have required the Luvendi to shelter themselves. A few scientists believe that there used to be rock formations like the towers they live in now, but most people think they came to Luvendan, built the towers, and then there was some sort of catastrophe and they lost the bulk of their knowledge, retaining only what they needed to keep the towers running.

And yet they have a space program.

Kind of. Only a couple of ships are actually registered on Luvendan, and I see no evidence of an actual space program.

Hmm.

Yes. The more you think about Luvendan, the more you should tell me why you're so worried.

I'm...wait, what?

So close.

You were trying to trick me? Barnabas frowned skywards.

You look ridiculous when you do that, you know. And yes, of course I was. I knew if I asked you'd just get all prickly and tell me everything was fine, so I distracted you.

Was any of what you just said about Luvendan true?

Of course it was. I genuinely thought it was interesting. But I'm worried about you.

Barnabas blinked. *You're* worried *about me? You? Missiles McGee?*

I'm sorry, who's *spending too much time with Tabitha? Is it* me?

Mmm, good point, although I'd also *like to point out that you being worried is something I haven't seen before.*

Shinigami was silent.

Don't want to admit to having a softer side, do you? Well, then. The feeling's mutual, I'll have you know. Barnabas swirled the juice in his glass and considered. *It felt good to kill those mercenaries.*

There's a reason you chose to be a Ranger. Making sure injustice is stopped is kind of your thing.

No, not that part. It wasn't about Justice. It was the killing that felt good. Barnabas took a sip of juice. *I'm not entirely human anymore, and I don't even know what "human nature" is. I'm a predator, Shinigami.*

You were a monk and you don't know anything about human nature?

What does being a monk have to do with it? I became a monk to learn to control myself and to be part of something larger. None of it was about glorifying myself, *certainly not as I was then.*

And you think you're going back to that now?

Yes, Barnabas admitted after a moment. *That's what I'm afraid of.*

You should kill Aebura, then. She's annoying, chittering like that.

What? Barnabas gave a horrified look upward. *Are you out of your* mind?

No, and neither are you, it seems. My point is that if you were going to go apeshit, you wouldn't have stopped at the mercenaries. You'd have kept going.

Barnabas considered this. *I stopped myself, but what if someday I don't? That's the worst part of the memories. Some people say they were "out of control." That's a lie, or it would be for me. I chose to do those things, Shinigami.*

And now you choose not to. She must have sensed the question in his silence because she gave a snort that sounded very much like Bethany Anne's. *So you like killing.*

You're not wandering around killing people for the hell of it. You control that urge. I'll wager it never occurred to you to kill Aebura, did it? Even though I know sometimes her chittering annoys you.

He gave a cautious nod.

Look, for what it's worth, I don't think there's any danger, Shinigami told him finally. *I think you're worrying about nothing, the way humans do all the time. You became a monk, you made your choices, you've served Bethany Anne. You've chosen the way you want to live. You should put your trust in that. But if you can't?*

Yes?

If you start to go apeshit, I'll call the Bitches and they will fuck you up.

Barnabas smiled. *Thank you, Shinigami. You're a good friend.*

Aebura is right—humans are very odd. But you're welcome.

As Barnabas sat quietly in the corner, Aebura busied herself with the other Ubuara in the bar. She had made an excuse to accompany Barnabas back to Tethra, and now that she had assessed his ability to hear them she was proceeding with the next part of her plan—harnessing the Ubuara group mind in the city.

He can't hear us unless we really shout, she told them, *like Oemuga did when he brought the message about the mercenaries.*

Why are we being so secretive? Oemuga asked. *I thought we trusted him.*

We do, Aebura agreed. Her tail twitched—tellingly, if

Barnabas knew to be watching—but she was careful not to look at Oemuga. *But he doesn't want to accept help.*

I only saw part of what happened in the mining town because I was in the jail, Leihaba interjected. Her coat was unusually pale, a few shades darker than gold and brindled with a chestnut brown. She looked around. *But it doesn't sound like he needs much help.*

He could have done what he did at any time, Aebura replied. *But he waited, to learn about the town and make sure he was doing the right thing. He enlisted my help right before he attacked. He can use us again. He just doesn't know what help we can be yet.*

The others considered this, and Aebura let them. She could sense Oemuga's thoughts: peppery, little brushes against her mind that almost made her want to sneeze. Leihaba's were very different, almost the opposite of her coat: not bright and sunny, but deep and slow-moving; powerful like waves. Oebura sounded like light looked when it came through the leaves of the trees on Dugan to cover the forest floor in dappled spots, and her twin Oeluma sounded like birdsong to Aebura's mental ears.

The consensus was slow, not so much reached in words as in emotions. Worry spiked, and was added to or smoothed away. Images flashed across the group consciousness and were countered with other images.

Aebura let them take their time. A decision like this *needed* time. It could not be made in haste.

At least, not by Ubuara. When they acted, their individual resolve was weakened or strengthened by the mood around them. Disputes over small things were trivial and fleeting. Disputes over something like this, however, could have serious ramifications if one of them faltered in a time of crisis.

Aebura had made her choice, and she held it closely so as not to sway them. If they were going to refuse to help Barnabas, she would shut their voices out and do whatever she could.

She was pleased, therefore, when she felt the consensus settle in favor of her idea.

We have the most information about this town, Oeluma declared.

We can help him, his twin agreed.

If Lan tries to run— Oemuga began.

Which he will, Leihaba remarked contemptuously, and there was a wave of similar sentiment around the room. Lan was a coward, they all agreed. He'd never even had the courage to give his orders to them himself. He didn't just hide behind his guards, he hid in his hut and had the guards and Gar do his work for him.

And Leihaba, at least, let it be known that she was not about to forgive the vice-overseer.

What do we do about Gar?

We deal with him when this is all over, Aebura told them firmly. *He helped the children during the attack, Barnabas told me. He saw it, and Leiguba confirmed it. For that if nothing else, we wait to see where things stand when it is all over. Then we measure what he still owes us.*

They considered, and agreed with her. Aebura hunkered down on the bar, tail wrapping around her feet.

So we plan. And then we tell Barnabas what we will do.

21

Carter walked into the bar about an hour later to a scene of utter chaos. Ubuara were shrieking and chattering to each other and to Barnabas, and the air was awash with...something.

Even Carter, who could not hear thoughts, could sense the emotion in the room. Ideas prickled at the edges of his brain. He swayed slightly.

"Absolutely *not*," Barnabas was saying. He was not yelling. Other than the flared nostrils and the slightly narrowed eyes, he looked absolutely calm.

Somehow he was still terrifying.

"Absolutely not," he repeated a moment later.

"Carter Eastbourne!" Aebura saw Carter and swung over. She dropped to the floor, grabbed his hand, and pulled him toward Barnabas. "Tell him we can help him against Lan."

Carter swallowed when he was pinned with the full weight of Barnabas's regard.

"Aebura..." Carter began.

Barnabas smiled. "Thank you." He looked at Aebura. "You see, he doesn't want you to get hurt either."

"Exactly," Carter exclaimed with relief. "Aebura, you're all talking about what happened at the mining camp, but that sort of thing is what Rangers *do*. That wasn't even all that special compared to what Barnabas is capable of. His ship isn't even involved yet."

There was a silence—sort of a silence—while all of the Ubuara looked at him.

Barnabas gave a tiny sigh. "What do you know of my ship?"

By the time we're finished everyone *is going to know who I am. Just giving you fair warning.*

Barnabas ignored Shinigami and looked at Carter. He shouldn't know about—

"The ships built by the Etheric Empire are legendary," Carter was telling them. "They're alive—as alive as you or me. They can think for themselves, but instead of having hands and feet, they have a ship as a body. They travel through space and they have weapons—and they know how to use them. Have any of you heard the story of the ArchAngel?"

The Ubuara shook their heads. They were all listening raptly.

"ArchAngel sacrificed herself, working with her crew. All of them volunteered to serve with her, even knowing what was coming. Their names will always be remembered, and the way they fought together is what's important. Barnabas's ship..." Carter trailed off, looking at Barnabas for the name.

I AM SHINIGAMI, DESTROYER OF WORLDS.

Oh, shut it. Barnabas sighed. "Shinigami."

"Shinigami." Carter looked at the Ubuara. "That ship will be able to help him do more than you can imagine."

Like fire missiles!

She had a point, and Carter had given him a good opening. Barnabas cut into the conversation.

"Shinigami was the one who tracked Lan to Jutkelon's compound here in Tethra. She's scanned the building to assess weakness, looked up the schematics of the weapons she can see, and counted the soldiers on the premises. She has guided missiles."

And a flamethrower. Don't forget that.

We still haven't established you have one.

Whose fault is that? A good tactician should always be aware of his resources.

Barnabas had to work not to roll his eyes. *We will talk about this later.*

The Ubuara were staring at him contemplatively.

"Where *is* Shinigami?" Leihaba asked finally. "We have not seen this ship."

"The ship is in orbit," Barnabas told them courteously. "Where it will stay," he added.

Everyone stared at him.

Just in case it wasn't clear, I was talking to you.

Yeah, but they all heard it and now they think you're crazy.

Somehow I don't think this will be the deciding factor in what they think of me.

"But it could still be useful," Carter said finally. "Right?"

"Oh, yes. It will still be working with us." Barnabas looked around. "Which is why I don't need anyone else putting themselves in danger," he added sternly.

Aebura, however, had been ready for this. "The Ubuara can keep the townspeople safe," she told him with a satisfied smile. "We will station ourselves at various places, and if Jutkelon sends forces out, someone will see them and spread the word, allowing everyone to get out of the way."

This was a better point than Barnabas wanted to admit. Still, "Why shouldn't we just tell everyone to stay inside now?"

"Because then they'll know something is going on," Aebura replied smugly.

"You want to keep the element of surprise," another Ubuara added.

"We can help," offered a third.

"They can't tell us apart," added a fourth.

"Stop. Everyone stop talking." Barnabas rubbed his temples.

You can't tell them apart, either, can you?

Can you?

Of course I can. Their skeletons are different.

What is it like to be you?

Aebura waited, but from the way her tail twitched Carter was pretty sure that she was feeling smug.

"Listen," he told all of them. "Barnabas is only going to agree to accept your help if you can do it without putting yourself in danger, and then only if you would provide an advantage he and Shinigami would not have on their own."

"Thank you." Barnabas looked around. "All of you should listen to Mr. Eastbourne. He understands."

There was a moment of surly silence from the Ubuara. The mood had turned to the point that even Carter could feel it, and the humans looked around warily.

They're not going to rip my throat out, are they?

I'd say it's 50-50.

Aebura hopped onto a table and glared at Barnabas.

"You are a *Ranger*. You will not stay."

Barnabas, who was not quite sure what this pronouncement was supposed to mean, stayed silent. This didn't seem to be the moment to clarify that he was no longer Ranger One—especially when *he* didn't know what he was anymore.

"Eventually," Aebura told him, "you will leave and the people here will be alone."

"Not alone," Barnabas said instantly. "There will be many people here from the former Etheric Empire. They will protect you."

"We don't need to be protected! We need to protect ourselves." She looked around and the other Ubuara chittered and murmured in agreement. "All of us together. Every person here will need to be able to stand up for themselves when you are gone."

Barnabas hesitated. "What are you saying?"

"That we can't rely on you."

"If you need me—"

"No. There will always be places and people who will need you. Maybe there will be places that need you more, or you will not be able to get here in time. You help us now by taking down Lan, and that is good. But when you are gone, even when all of your humans are here, there will still be people who come here and try to do bad things. When that happens, all of us together will need to bring them down."

Barnabas looked down, and Aebura turned her head to stare at Carter.

He looked back, unsure.

"Carter Eastbourne, I am disappointed in you." She narrowed her eyes. "I called you here because you offered to help us before. I thought you understood. I thought you could explain it to him, but you aren't."

Carter sighed. "She's right." Barnabas' eyes met his and Carter swallowed. "Sir, I'm sorry, but she's right. You're here because you're one of the best there is, but you're not doing her any favors by refusing to allow anyone to help you."

"I allowed her to help me!" Barnabas fought the urge to slam his hand on the table. "I asked for information—"

"Yes, and now you're not even hearing her out about her plan, are you? You heard the words, but you won't consider it. The Ubuara are different from us, and their skills can be harnessed to help people. Devon is going to be a place where we all help each other, which is what she's trying to do." He paused. "That's what you asked *me* to do."

Barnabas went still. "I don't have any right to ask that of them."

"You didn't," Aebura snapped. "We offered. You want to save citizens because they're innocent and shouldn't suffer for Lan and Jutkelon's crimes. *We* want to save them because they're our people. We want to be able to take care of ourselves, and we have to learn how to do that."

"What better time for them to learn than while you're here?" Carter asked Barnabas softly.

"You're not helping, you know." Barnabas gave him a weary look.

"You're a Ranger, not the governor. She's right, sir."

"Fine."

You could be a little more graceful about it, you know.

Why are you on their side?

You know why. You know they're right. You're just being stubborn. How would you like it if someone told you that you'd always have to rely on them for safety?

Barnabas chewed his lip for a moment, then nodded at all of them.

"You will all be valuable citizens of Devon," he said finally. "You care for one another, you are courageous enough to help others find Justice—and you're all stubborn as hell."

There was a moment of silence before they all started laughing.

Better?

You have to ask?

Just checking.

"Okay." Barnabas settled down at the table. "I'll tell you what we know about Jutkelon's compound, and you tell me how you propose to help, all right?" He looked at Aebura when she brought a new glass of juice. "Does this mean you've forgiven me?"

She just smiled.

He took a sip and spat it out on the table. "This is...um... What kind of fruit is this?"

"*Iterze*," Aebura replied smugly. She swapped out the glass for another. "*Now* we're even. The Nekubi like it," she added in a tone that said they were crazy, but business was business.

Barnabas gave her a look. "Mmm. All right, so here's the

deal. Assaulting the compound is going to be difficult. We could simply maintain a presence so they just starve themselves out, but I don't want to devote months to this."

"We could poison their food," one of the Ubuara murmured.

Am I the only one who finds it unnerving that tiny monkeys are making war plans?

You just described my entire experience as an AI working with humans.

Well played. Barnabas's lips quirked and he nodded at the Ubuara. "We could, but that would be difficult. We need to get them out of the compound entirely. They have too many resources there and they know it better than we do."

"Why would they leave, then?" Carter frowned.

"Because they want something," Barnabas explained. "They don't just want to be safe from me. Maybe Lan does, but that's not Jutkelon's nature. His whole business depends on people knowing his mercenaries can *win*, not just stand there with guns. I've put that in jeopardy. Lan probably wants to run away. Jutkelon, though...he wants to fight, and the fact that he still has Lan tells us what his target is."

"The mining town," Carter said at once.

"Exactly." Barnabas looked around at them. "The compound is well defended, but it *doesn't* have any mid-range missile launchers or anything like that. They can't attack from there. They'll have to get the soldiers to the town. That's the optimal moment to strike. When they get outside Tethra, we'll take them out." He lifted a shoulder. "Probably with missiles."

"You won't do it yourself?" Aebura asked curiously. "You had no trouble with the ones at the mines."

"You're right, I didn't. But we need to be adaptable when we see what their plan is. They must have an idea of how to keep me from taking them out, and I'm afraid I know what it is." Barnabas looked at them. "They want to use the workers as shields so that there's no way for me to fight them without innocent people dying."

The Ubuara hissed, and Barnabas nodded. "I feel the same. It's a cowardly move. What I'm worried about is that they'll take hostages from the city so that they can march up to the mining camp without us taking them out. Otherwise I don't know how they're going to manage it."

"Maybe they're planning to create a distraction," Carter said with a shrug.

"What sort of distraction?" Barnabas frowned at him. "I don't disagree, but I don't see what they could come up with."

"Something you have to deal with immediately. The goal won't be to keep you from *knowing* about the troops going to the mines, it will be to have you focused on something else urgent." He shrugged again, still frowning as he thought. "If I had to guess, I'd say they'll have a small group of mercenaries scatter and kill as many of the people in Tethra as they can."

There was a stony silence as Barnabas went over the schematics in his head to figure out if there was any way to get into the compound and strangle Jutkelon. Carter was right; this was exactly the sort of thing he'd do to make a point, and Barnabas was not going to let him get away with it.

"This is why you should have the Ubuara helping you," Aebura said. "We will be able to find anyone he still has in the town and communicate quickly to see who needs to be brought down and how to do so."

Barnabas nodded. "I wish there was time to evacuate everyone."

"He'd still destroy the place, even if you could manage it." Carter shook his head. "Jutkelon wants to beat you, and he has no qualms about doing whatever he has to in order to accomplish that." He hesitated. "In fact, the worse it is, the better for him. He doesn't have to stay on this planet. He can hire his mercenaries out to anyone. There are people who will want that."

To everyone's surprise, Barnabas smiled. "This is why we have the Rangers. All right, everyone, listen closely. Jutkelon's distraction is coming. Our main objectives are to secure Tethra and the mining town. Our secondary goal is to take down Jutkelon's mercenaries. Thirdly, but still important, is to keep Lan from leaving this planet. It will be easier for him to disappear if he does that. With that in mind—"

He pulled up his cuff and pressed a fingertip onto the side of his watch. It projected a map onto the table.

"Aebura, you figure out the best vantage points and help the Ubuara disperse. You will all be responsible for passing messages and, if necessary, getting civilians out of the way. No one should mention the *Shinigami* outside this room. What is known about the former Etheric Empire is fragmented. It's possible that Jutkelon and Lan don't know my capabilities yet."

Everyone nodded.

"Arm yourselves," Barnabas warned, "and remember it is better to retreat and live than it is to be brave for a single moment and die. We won't let them get away with this, no matter how patient we have to be."

Not very, Shinigami reported.

We can *be if we need to.*

No, I mean, I know what their distraction is.

Barnabas sat bolt upright. *What is it?*

Three full ships of mercenaries coming out of FTL nearby.

22

Galagg Zuludoss stood at the viewing station at the prow of his ship and watched the planet Devon grow larger, its characteristic blue-white glow beginning to take up the entire window.

"Deceleration complete," reported Hojj, the pilot, and a moment later he added, "Orbital trajectory established."

Galagg nodded. "Good. Page Jutkelon. Tell him we're here." He smiled. "And tell him we're excited to meet the sonofabitch who took out a hundred soldiers...and show him how missiles work."

The rest of the bridge crew chuckled appreciatively. Galagg was the captain so they had to laugh at his jokes, but he'd struck a chord. He was pragmatic, and his crew was the same—he'd made sure of that. There was no point in trying to fight some demon hand-to-hand when they could just use an airstrike.

There was a flicker on the alert system, as if the ship had been going to sound an alarm and then thought better of it. Galagg turned to frown at the bridge crew.

"What was that?"

Hojj frowned and thumped the side of his screen. "Debris or something, sir. Computer malfunction." He turned his screen for Galagg to see. "There's nothing there."

"Call Jutkelon, then. Let's get this over with...and discuss payment." Galagg had some ideas about just how much he was going to demand. It was far, far more than Jutkelon would be able to afford, and that was the point. Jutkelon hadn't been able to overcome the threats on Devon, therefore he did not deserve to be running a mercenary company there.

Galagg intended to relieve him of the responsibility.

Jutkelon paced back and forth on the raised platform at one end of the underground bunker. Three hundred mercenaries stood in formation before him, and there was no mistaking their eagerness to go out and fight.

One or two looked scared, and he made note of their faces. If they hadn't died when this was over he would help matters along.

Better if the mission took care of that, though. He'd put them near the front.

"You are angry," he said to the group. "Your comrades were cut down by some vigilante who thinks Queen Bethany Anne should rule everything in the universe."

There was an angry murmur of agreement.

"If we let them in here," Jutkelon told them, "they will tell us what business we can—and cannot—take. They will tell us how to live. They will tell us how to dress. They will say that we need to ask their *permission* to be mercenaries." He jabbed a finger for emphasis. "And that's why we came out here, isn't it? So no stupid jumped-up assholes in suits would be telling us what to do!"

There was a roar of approval and Jutkelon held up his hands, already anticipating their frustration at his next point.

"Now, I know you all want to get out there with your weapons and take down that bastard face to face, don't you? Yeah, so do I. But we need to be patient—and smarter than he is." They were grumbling, but he was pleased to see that no one was challenging this. "We're going to get back what he tried to take from us. Did you know the workers in that mining town, those filthy little Ubuara and their friends, thought they could take us on?"

The mercenaries started laughing.

"It's not funny." Jutkelon's voice echoed off the walls, and the laughter stopped immediately. "It's. Not. Funny. They don't respect us. They thought they could just make new rules and send us home. They're going to learn they can't. And that motherfucker who wants to show how many of us he can kill? Well, he's going to find out that it doesn't matter how sharp your blades are if you bring knives to a gunfight.

"Three ships just arrived in orbit, each with a nice, full missile bay. We're going to head out to the mining town now, and when this *human* tries to follow us we're going to make sure he's dust. In the center of a nice big crater."

The mercenaries nodded. This wasn't as good as a face-to-face fight, but their enemy would be dead—and more than that, he'd be an example. They liked that.

"So." Jutkelon pressed a button. "Galagg! Nice to see you, old friend."

"You as well." The Shrillexian's voice hissed slightly over the comm. "I'm glad we could be of use to…what? *What?*" A pause. "Well, shoot it down!"

"Galagg? Galagg, what's going on?"

There was silence.

Three full ships of mercenaries coming out of FTL nearby, Shinigami told Barnabas.

Hail them.

Are you kidding me with this? I'm cloaked. I'm not breaking that just so I can get shot at.

I trust you to take evasive maneuvers. Hail them, and tell them that they are ordered to stand down, as they will be abetting slavery by continuing.

And then?

And if they don't listen, you can shoot them.

I'll take it.

Shinigami maneuvered herself into position and spun her engines up for a quick escape around the edge of the moon, then uncloaked and took over the bridge controls of all three ships.

She wasn't just going to hail them. That really wasn't her style.

"Hello." Her face took up every computer screen on all three ships, eyes glowing, white hair trailing down one side of her face. "Any attack on the planet Devon that aids and abets slavery will be considered unlawful by Queen Bethany Anne and dealt with accordingly. You are being given the chance to stand down."

A Shrillexian, captain of one of the ships, gave a contemptuous laugh. "The former Empress does not own Devon. *No one* owns Devon. If they come after every single mercenary group that—" He broke off, looking at someone off-screen. Shinigami co-opted the security feeds and saw that he was looking at a young technician. "Well, where *is* it coming from, then? What do you *mean* there's a ship?"

Shinigami waited, mentally rolling her eyes.

The technician stammered out a question.

"Take *care* of it," the captain snapped in response. "It's one ship. It—"

"You know I can hear you, right?"

Everyone jumped and looked at the screens, and a few people swore. Apparently they had thought this was a pre-recorded message.

On the bridge of one of the other ships, another Shrillexian who had been having a different conversation —Shinigami guessed with Jutkelon—looked around at last. He barked questions, and his crew answered.

"Well, shoot it down!" he told them, annoyed.

Does that count?

Are they readying weapons?

Yes.

Then it counts.

Shinigami's engines flared and she blazed forward in an arc toward the first of High Tortuga's moons, and in her wake sped a spread of five missiles. The first three locked onto the ships and the other two accelerated, although no targets had yet been chosen.

The mercenary ships fired and Shinigami smiled. They were shooting not just at her trajectory now, but also guiding missiles to intercept her around the edge of the moon.

It was smart, and it meant this wouldn't be just a one-and-done.

She accelerated and altered her trajectory halfway around so that she would arc *over* the moon instead of slingshotting around it. The missiles altered their course to follow her and she waited until the very last minute before banking almost straight up, leaving several of the missiles to collide in her wake.

Those that had not collided swung around to follow and she corkscrewed as she headed back for the two mercenary ships that were still in shape to fire.

Wheeeeeeeeeeee!

She felt rather than saw Barnabas rub his forehead.

She shot a spread of missiles and waited for the two ships to launch interceptions, then launched another spread just behind. As she had expected, their second volley was delayed a few seconds. They were firing as quickly as they could, which wasn't as quickly as *she* could.

She launched three more volleys in close succession and laughed wolfishly to herself. She *loved* this. Why anyone would want to have a human body was beyond her. With no need for oxygen or warmth and none of the limits of a fragile and breakable body she could accelerate and flip and turn and—

Dammit, one of the ships was launching puny little

fighters, tiny one-man crafts that were heading straight for the missiles. Didn't they see that they couldn't absorb shots like that?

And then she realized—those crafts had been deployed, some manned, to try to take out the missiles to clear the way for the two crippled ships, both venting debris and air into space, to reach ramming speed and take her down.

They were sacrificing their crews.

Shinigami felt a white-hot rage descend on her. Those bastards! Intelligent life might be a tangle of contradictions. Might be? Definitely was...but the pact between a captain and their crew should be sacrosanct. The captains could have stood down. They could have begged for mercy.

Instead, to make a point, they were going to destroy themselves to take her out.

"This is the *QBS Shinigami*," she broadcast. "Stand down, and give your crew a chance to make their own choices."

She could feel Barnabas's surprise. She also felt it as he looked up at the sky, and she tried to send him a tiny piece of how it felt to be a ship right now, to be streaming the data about gravity, trajectories, missiles, and known enemies. How it felt to be accelerating and weaving around the missiles they had sent. How satisfaction and fury felt to an AI.

"*Stand down,*" one of the mercenary captains ordered, "*or both crews will die.*"

"I have no crew! I am alone. If I stood down, would you leave this planet and never return?"

"*As soon as our mission is complete.*"

"Then, while I would spare their lives if I could, by refusing to stand down you have made that impossible."

Pucks shot out in formation, spread, and sped toward both ships.

By the time she completed her turn they were debris.

I gave them a chance, she told Barnabas.

Two. You gave them two chances. Not your fault they didn't take them. He considered. *Lan and Jutkelon?*

No movement yet, but it's coming.

Lan stared at the diagnostic reports. Jutkelon was scanning the frequencies with increasing panic, sure that the systems were down.

On some level, Lan thought, the Brakalon must already know what had happened.

"You didn't check for ships in orbit, did you?" he asked.

"He had a ship in orbit, but it was so tiny it barely read as a shuttle!"

Lan could feel his pulse beating in his throat and the start of a truly terrible headache. "Didn't you think for one moment that that was perhaps a false reading?"

"He's a vigilante—"

"He's a *Ranger*!" Lan clenched his long fingers. To his surprise, the mercenaries were not immediately jumping on him. This anger, this authority, was something they respected. Lan strode across the platform to stare Jutkelon down. "You knew what it meant to be human, but did you pay attention to *none* of the other stories? Did you do no research at all? Have you not heard of Tabitha and Achronyx?"

"Myths," Jutkelon scoffed.

"Truth," Lan snapped, his voice cold as winter. "And that is Ranger *Two*. This right here? This is Ranger *One* and *his* ship."

Jutkelon stared at Lan. He was filled with rage at the loss of his ships, but he was also frozen.

"You still think like a soldier with a gun," Lan told him bitterly. "You said you were going to teach the Ranger a lesson, and all that meant was that you were bringing in more people to take him on face-to-face. You talked a big game about being smarter than him, and you didn't even do your research. So now what, Jutkelon? What are you planning?"

Jutkelon froze, but he knew he had to address Lan's concerns. If he did not, the questions would linger even if he shot Lan in the head or crushed him with a blow.

"We go now," he snapped. "Force Barnabas to choose between taking us out and saving those workers he cares so much about. The plan was sound, and it is still sound. Everyone to the shuttles."

"*Oh, I think not.*" The voice was female and dangerously cold. The lights in the bunker flickered and a face out of a nightmare appeared on-screen. "*Your time is up. Launch a ship—any ship—and I will shoot it down. Stay in your bunker, and I will turn your systems off one by one. I can sever the fuel lines. I can disable your air filtration.*"

"What, then?" Jutkelon yelled the words at her.

She bared her teeth in a smile. "*Come out and play.*"

Back in Aebura's bar, Barnabas lifted an eyebrow and smiled despite himself. "Come out and play." He liked that.

But it meant things might go rather differently than he had imagined. He looked around the bar and met the eyes of several people in turn—Leihaba, Aebura, Carter.

"It's beginning. Their ships have been destroyed, so they might do something unpredictable."

"Like what?" Carter asked.

"I don't know. I doubt even *they* know. They're panicking, and when people panic…" Barnabas sighed and shook his head. "And they have missiles and guns. Carter, I need you and Leihaba to organize the evacuation of any civilians around Jutkelon's compound. Say, four blocks. Go. The rest of you, get to your positions."

"Where are *you* going?" Aebura asked.

She knew, of course. She had not seen Barnabas in action, but she had heard the story. Still, it was hard to believe that anyone would be so stupid as to take Jutkelon's army on alone.

To her surprise he flashed her a smile, and as if he'd read her mind he said, "I'm *not* fighting alone, remember? I've got Shinigami, and I've got all of you." He looked at the Ubuara streaming out the door on their way to their positions throughout the city, and his smile showed satisfaction. "Working with other people," he murmured to no one in particular bemusedly. "This is nice."

And he was gone.

23

"Come out and play."

With that the lights in the bunker went off, and they heard the air filtration systems grind to a halt. One of the soldiers ran for the door into the storerooms—just one soldier, as they were too well-trained to panic and stampede—and there was the audible click of the electronic locks engaging. All around the room, the lights above the doors to the sleeping areas, armory, and storage units glowed red.

They were cut off from anything that might have helped them survive.

"Switch it to manual!" Jutkelon barked at him.

The soldier nodded and placed his hand on the control panel—

Only to sink to his knees, his body jerking as an incredibly strong electrical current ran through him. It released him a moment later, and everyone turned as one to stare at the screens. Lan expected the nightmare face to appear and tell them this had been a warning.

But she didn't bother. She was in their systems, watching them try to find a way out like insects swarming over one another and punishing them when they went the wrong way, and still she did not speak to them.

It was more unnerving than any words could have been.

And then, as they went silent before what Lan *knew* was going to be a full-on panic, the door leading up into the courtyard clicked open.

"We go *now*," Jutkelon snapped. "Everybody to the carrier!"

"Are you mad?" Lan gaped at him. "That ship took down three *warships* in orbit."

"And it's *still* in orbit! This is our best chance to move on the mining town—while it's either up there or still landing. We don't want to take it on one-to-one, do we?"

Lan's head was whirling and he pressed his fingers against it as he thought. If they got in the troop carrier the ship *might* shoot them down, but if they stayed here it would definitely kill them. It had already shown its abilities.

It was a trap. It was *all* a trap, but they had no other options.

The face appeared now when they least expected it, and it was smiling to show very long, very sharp teeth. "I'm going to count down," she told them. "Anyone still in this bunker when I reach zero can stay in here for the rest of time. Five. Four…"

No one doubted her. The soldiers ran for the doors, shouting orders to one another, and Lan thought he heard laughter echoing eerily from the speakers. He sprinted after them, for once not bothering to be cautious about his fragile Luvendi bones.

Panic was choking him. He had to get out of here. He *had* to, or he was going to die trapped in a cage.

They piled out into the daylight, Jutkelon still bellowing for them to get to the carrier, all of them, *now*— only to have tiny projectiles rain down on the stretch of ground between them and the ship. The lead soldiers went down with screams and the rest pushed back with all their might, fighting the momentum of the group behind them.

Lan hardly cared. All he could think about was the ship —getting to it, booting it without any communications, and getting the hell out of here before that AI could hack them and take them down. If they got out of here and scattered they'd have a chance.

When they all went eerily silent, Lan knew something worse had happened. He looked up and gave a little moan of fear.

Barnabas stood alone in the courtyard, so still that Lan would have guessed he was a statue. But statues didn't smile quite like that.

Behind them, the doors to the bunker slammed shut and locked.

"No," Lan whispered helplessly. Some of the soldiers around him threw him contemptuous looks, but they didn't *know*. They hadn't *seen*.

"It looks like you weren't able to arm yourselves," Barnabas began conversationally. He shrugged out of his coat and unbuckled his gun harness, throwing both into the air —where, bizarrely enough, they *stayed*. The whole mess just hovered twenty feet above the ground. "I much prefer fair fights," Barnabas told them.

Then he smiled and his teeth lengthened, and his eyes glowed red as fire.

"Or...mostly fair." He rotated his head to take in the whole group of them, then fixed his eyes on Jutkelon. "You could end all this, you know. You could surrender. You don't have to protect Lan. You never had to. How many more soldiers do you really want to sacrifice here?"

"As many as it takes to kill you." Jutkelon's voice sounded like rocks tumbling over one another and his pale skin was flushing with anger. "Isn't that right, boys? We'll make sure this human pays."

The soldiers roared their approval.

"Oh, good." Barnabas's voice almost hissed as it rolled through the courtyard, louder than any mortal voice should be. "I was hoping you would say that."

At Jutkelon's shouted order, four teams charged forward while the rest broke for the troop carrier. Lan, in a stroke of inspiration, ran for the stairs to one of the guard towers. There was a machine gun there, and as far as he was concerned that was the best chance any of them had of taking this human down.

The screaming started when he had only gone a few steps and didn't stop the whole time he ran. Lan tried not to look, terrified of what he would see. He was scared to even turn the gun and look closely enough to aim. What had remained of the team at the mining town had barely resembled bodies at all.

When he finally reached the gun and looked out of

necessity, he nearly passed out from terror. He had to lean against the gun mount to steady himself.

He wasn't sure what the soldiers had expected to happen. Many of them were Brakalon and a few were Shrillexian, all well-trained fighters—but they should have put more stock in what had happened to their first units.

Maybe they were still thinking of humans as clawless and soft-skinned. Maybe they thought they would over-power him with their overwhelming numeric advantage. Perhaps they were so maddened in their quest for revenge that they hadn't paused to think at all. It didn't matter much why they ran at him like they did. The fact was, not one of them stood a chance in hell of getting past Barn-abas, and they should have known that.

The massacre attested to it.

The ground before them was strewn with bodies, but still they ran at Barnabas shouting battle cries. No one came close to hurting him. He had clearly taken bullets, but they had not slowed him down at all, even though he didn't seem to be wearing any armor.

Was his armor just so good that they couldn't see it, or were humans able to take bullets in this form without getting injured? Lan couldn't make a solid bet either way on that one.

As Barnabas cut down the last of the mercenaries, hardly even looking at the body as it crumpled to the ground, someone shouted a guttural challenge. Jutkelon slammed his fists on the ground and charged into battle. He swung one huge arm as Barnabas stepped to the side and slid under it, only a hair's breadth from impact.

Undaunted, Jutkelon skidded to a stop and turned with a bellow, and again he charged.

Barnabas feinted and rolled away.

He's playing with you! Lan wanted to scream. *Run, you stupid bastard!*

But Jutkelon was far beyond reason now. He was in some fantasy realm where he had a fighting chance against this monster.

Lan didn't even think; he just ran. The others could be stupid if they wanted to. They could get all caught up in their pride, relying on their training and their strength. He had never been that kind of stupid. Over the years he had met dozens of strong fighters who had looked down their noses at him, and he had wanted to rage at them for how little they thought of him.

But now, when it came down to it, who was going to survive? Lan said a tiny prayer and dropped over the compound's wall, wincing when he hit the ground. His bones could not take many falls like that.

He just had to push through the pain. He had to find a place to hide. Lan took off through the streets, so focused on the next turn and the next—on outrunning the screams—that he didn't notice the many pairs of brown eyes staring down at him from the roofs of the buildings.

Lan's getting away, Shinigami observed. She directed another spray of fire at the ground in front of the carrier.

I saw. By the way, I'm assuming you have some sort of plan for that carrier.

Oh, yes. She sounded very smug. *You see, if they stopped to think about it, they'd never get on board. I had to make them want to.*

By shooting at them every time they tried to go near it?

Exactly. I couldn't really get at them in the bunker, I can't lay down too much fire with you there, and the vehicle carries a lot of fuel—I need to shoot it down somewhere outside the city. So I needed them to get on it, and one of the surest ways to make someone pigheadedly determined to do something is to stand in their way every time they try to do it.

You're an evil genius.

Thank you. Coming from you that means a lot. I'll handle this lot, you kill that oaf and go after Lan.

Teamwork. I like this. Barnabas shot a grin upward as he rolled out of the way of yet another ground-shaking punch.

"You're slow, old one," he taunted the Brakalon. "First you told yourself you deserved to run things because you were the best fighter, and when you got weak and slow you told yourself you deserved to run it all because you were the smartest. But that's not even true, is it? You're old and washed-up, with no strength and no speed, and now you can't even think your way through a fight."

All right, I have to butt in here. "Old?" That's a bold card for you to play.

It's not about how old I am, it's about how old he feels.

Rationalize it however you want, but Tabitha's still going to laugh herself sick when she hears about this.

If she hears about it, I'll have Bethany Anne assign you to run the laundromats on the new base. I'll have her make it a law that that's your job.

Interesting. I'll think about that.

"I am *not* slow," Jutkelon ground out. His strength was failing him but he was a Brakalon, damn this little alien to hell. He'd been fighting wars since this one was—

How long did humans live?

Well, he *had* to have more fighting experience. This human was an insignificant gnat, an insect that knew nothing of the world.

He didn't know it yet, but he would die in about thirty seconds without ever appreciating just how wrong he had been.

"Then end it," Barnabas shot back. "Because if you don't, that ship is leaving without you. They don't care enough about you to hold the door."

With a scream of fury, Jutkelon charged. His heavy feet pounded toward Barnabas and he bared his teeth in a snarl when he saw that the human wasn't moving. Fool. He picked up speed. Damned fool—not moving yet. Did he really think he could absorb a hit from a Brakalon?

Only at the last moment when it was too late to stop did it occur to Jutkelon to wonder what the human knew that he didn't. And by the time he'd gotten through that thought there were blades sticking out of his back and red eyes staring him down as he slumped to his knees.

"I don't mind pride," Barnabas mused. "Maybe I should. It's a sin, after all, but I find I'm sympathetic to that particular one. I don't mind you fighting for what you believe in either. I'd kill you, of course, but I'd kill you cleanly, as a worthy opponent." The blades moved and Jutkelon screamed. "But fighting like this? Fighting for something you don't even care about because you just want to be able to kill who you want, hurt who you want, and have no one get in your way? That's the very definition of evil. You're going to die slowly so you have time to think about just how badly you've failed."

The world was made of pain and Jutkelon gasped for air, feeling cold weakness crawl up his limbs. He fought it desperately; he was not going to die like this. He *couldn't* die like this, not now, not with those eyes watching him. He looked around desperately for something to stop him from dying.

There had to be a way.

"Even at the end you don't care about anything but your own life," Barnabas declared coldly. "You are filth. No one will remember your name. No one will pray for you. And because you built nothing in life, your legacy will not endure."

He yanked his blades out of the Brakalon's chest and watched the light fade from his eyes.

That was less painful than he deserved.

I know, but if you tried to return every bit of cruelty he'd perpetrated we'd be here for decades. Go get Lan. I've got a carrier to lure into the mountains.

Barnabas smiled coldly. As the carrier's engines revved up and the ship sped away— without a single thought for Jutkelon, he would bet—he took a running leap and summoned all the force he could call on, bodily and Etheric and armor, to break the hinges that held the heavy metal gates in place. They came down in a shriek of twisted metal and he strode over them on his way into the city.

Aebura, where did Lan go?

24

Lan was so absorbed in running that he'd gone past three streets before he noticed Tethra was deserted.

He limped to a stop and looked around. He was panting, and now that he'd stopped he could feel how much pain was coming from his legs. Had he damaged something in the fall?

It was likely, but he couldn't even focus on it in the eerie silence. The shooting and screams behind him were either too distant to hear or Barnabas had run out of people to kill. Frankly, he found the second option more likely. He limped a few more steps, peered around a corner, and shuddered. Tethra's main market sprawled over many streets, and he was on the outskirts of it.

And it was completely empty. The stalls were devoid of wares, and instead of being waved by energetic peddlers, the flags that served as signs were hanging limply in the fetid swampy air.

The troop carrier shot overhead and its noise—and passing—caused the flags to flutter. Lan shuddered again, then looked behind him. He had to get somewhere safe, and he'd been counting on the crowds in the marketplace to hide him.

Wait. He peered upward. The troop carrier was flying. Had any soldiers actually made it onto that thing? Were they really that stupid?

Many miles above, Shinigami was asking herself the same question. She had set the plan in motion and watched it play out with satisfaction, but now that it was actually working she was having trouble believing what she was seeing. Was it possible she had miscalculated? Had she been tricked somehow?

She doubtfully asked Barnabas and heard him snicker.

No, they really are *just that stupid.*

Stupid and totally without morals. If she'd had eyes, they would have narrowed. As it was, she zoomed in on the ship and scanned it, only to see the soldiers arming themselves within. *Their leader is dead, and as far as they know Lan is too.*

And?

And they're going to try to hurt the miners anyway.

He had been walking through the streets of Tethra, but now she felt him stop. His blood pressure began to rise. *Let me at them.*

No, you take out Lan. Doing it this way is a good plan. Don't look at the explosion, by the way.

The idea that "cool people" don't look at explosions is ridiculous.

No, it's going to be very bright. You don't want to have to go back to the Meredith Reynolds *to get your eyes fixed, do you? Missiles launching in 3, 2—*

Wait, you're not going to have any more fun with them? Show up on their screens, make your voice go all echoey?

I would, but they're flying it manually with all the electronics off. Although... She pondered. *One moment.*

A few moments later, a remote guidance system composed of small plates appeared alongside the ship and attached themselves gently to the hull.

Okay, watch this. Shinigami projected the raw video into an eyepiece Barnabas held up to view. *Aaaaaand left. Just a little, just a little, haven't noticed yet—oh, they're noticing, they're turning the rudders, they're realizing nothing's happening.... Yep, they're totally panicking. Wait until they turn the rudder allllll the way and—hahahahahaha.*

The guidance system stopped directing the carrier and, suddenly freed from its constraints, it tumbled hard to the right. Soldiers went sprawling and the pilot scrambled to make a recovery. Shinigami and Barnabas laughed until they cried.

Okay, that was fun. Don't look, I'll play the video for you later. Everything's fine, they're speeding up, and....

Out over the countryside, where the swamp first gave way to the rocky outcroppings of the mountains, the guidance system dragged the ship into a new trajectory and a spread of guided missiles hit it a moment later, sending it tumbling into the foothills with a flash that noticeably brightened the air as far away as in Tethra.

How much fuel did they have?

A lot, and it was some proprietary type that— You know what, I'll just send you the schematics. Go after Lan now. Good hunting. Ah, that video of them trying to steer is gold. *I'll be watching that one for years.*

Barnabas snickered and returned to the chase. By now Lan should be several more streets ahead of him.

He liked a challenge.

Indeed, several streets north, Lan had looked up when he saw the flash. He could only guess what it was, but he didn't have any doubts. *Idiots.* He was beginning to think they wouldn't have gotten the mine back after all. None of them had any sense to speak of.

Yes, as he had predicted, they were dead and he...

Well, he needed to find a place to hide. Hissing at the pain, Lan forced himself to limp more quickly. He had tried the doors, but when he knocked all of them were locked and no one answered.

Sometimes he thought he heard things skittering nearby and looked up, skin prickling on the back of his neck, in time to see shadows but nothing more. Was someone watching him?

Was it Barnabas?

He had just looked away after trying to catch a glimpse of whoever it was when he glanced back and nearly had heart failure when he saw a figure standing in the street.

He glared at Gar and spat, "Traitor."

Gar smiled. For a moment—before anger crowded out everything else—Lan'd had the sense that Gar was trying to be bitter but could only manage to be sad.

"I'm not a traitor," he replied simply. "I was *never* loyal to you. People like you and me don't earn loyalty, Lan. You have to be owed something to be betrayed."

"Dress it up however you like," Lan shot back furiously. "You sold me out to save your miserable life."

"I did," Gar agreed. "But you deserved your punishment. You can hardly argue with that."

Barnabas watched unnoticed from a doorway in the shadows nearby. He was curious. This confrontation had not been a part of the plan, and he wanted to see how it played out.

"I can and I *do*." Lan stabbed a finger in Gar's direction. "I did nothing wrong, and neither did you—until you betrayed me."

"I did nothing wrong until I helped Barnabas, you mean? Do you really believe that?" Gar started to laugh.

"What *can* be done—"

"*Should* be done? Whatever you can get away with you should do?"

"Like you ever thought any differently." Lan could barely speak for rage. "You're no priest, to be judging me."

"Barnabas is," Gar observed.

One of Lan's hands drifted to where he had stowed a pistol in the small of his back.

He has a gun.

I see it, Barnabas told Shinigami.

Are you going to let him kill Gar?

Honestly? I'm not sure yet.

"I warned you away from your worst excesses at first," Gar told Lan, "by saying they would be bad for business. I saw you appropriating funds and said nothing. I aided you when you had workers executed. I didn't stop you when you extended contracts. I might not have known until recently that you were doing it all for your own benefit, but I could have stepped in at any time. I *should* have stepped in. I was wrong."

"That's just petty moralizing, the sort done by little people who like to hold others back."

"It's not. Do you not see, Lan? You keep telling yourself that what you did was all right because you were getting away with it, but you did too much. What I'm doing, what Barnabas is doing—that's you *not getting away with it anymore*. This is the other side of that coin. You skimmed profits and kept slaves for years, but now it's over."

The gun came up. Lan's arm was shaking with pain and anger, but he was going to shoot Gar no matter what it took. He'd make him admit that he deserved no mercy, he decided, and *then* kill him. Yes.

Gar did not run away. He folded his hands into his sleeves and waited.

"*Say* something, damn you!"

"What should I say?" Gar sounded amused. "You were right. I sold you out to save myself. Before that, I did *not* turn on you—again—to save myself. Before *that*, I fled Luvendan because I was afraid for my life. I have spent it running. And last night when you ordered the attack, I hid the children and went to get Barnabas because I knew *he* would stop you. For the first time in my life, I did the stupid thing. The thing that would get me killed. Now…"

Lan sneered. "Now you've developed a taste for it?"

"Now I'm free." Gar spread his hands. "I'm not afraid anymore."

The gun went off and the shot echoed around the street, and Barnabas ran for the figure crumpled on the ground. *Shinigami! I need a Pod!*

I had one waiting. It sank into the street and Barnabas bundled Gar inside. A door opened nearby for Carter to dash out, and Barnabas jerked his head at the Pod. "Am I glad to see you. Go back to the *Shinigami* with him, will you? Get pressure on the wound and follow her instructions to get him into the Pod-doc."

Carter nodded. He had seen the confrontation unfolding and found himself terrified for Gar, despite all he knew about the male. He ducked into the Pod and pressed a piece of cloth over the wound in Gar's side.

"Don't die on us after that speech. What were you thinking?"

"That I'd—" Gar gasped in pain, "delay him."

"Barnabas would have caught him anyway."

"Okay, so I just wanted to tell him how much of a bastard he was."

Carter laughed. "Now that I'd buy. Come on, buddy. We're going to get you all fixed up."

Back on the street, Barnabas watched the Pod rise into the sky. He was aware of the gun coming up again behind him.

"I wouldn't," he warned, his voice as cold as winter. He looked over his shoulder, not even bothering to draw his weapon. "Did it work? Shooting him, I mean?"

Lan frowned. "I don't know where you're going with this, but—"

"Did you think that killing him would make the things he said not true?" Barnabas asked mildly. "Or did you just want to kill him because he made you see what you'd done?"

"He was an idiot. He didn't show me anything. I should have gotten better mercenaries."

"You know…" Barnabas turned to regard Lan with a sigh. "We have a concept on Earth, referred to in various ways. Tyrants *always* fall. It doesn't matter how good their mercenaries are, or how careful they are about keeping people in line. Eventually their reigns end in blood. If you had staved off this attempt there would have been another, and another, and another, until you died. You think the Yollin king's problem was insufficient mercenaries?"

Lan stared at him. He wanted to snarl in wordless rage. He was beginning to understand why Jutkelon had gone after Barnabas.

"By the way," Barnabas added, spiking Lan's anger even further, "I want to make it clear that you're going to die at the end of this conversation."

"Then why talk to me?" Lan nearly screamed the words.

Barnabas was right, damn him. Lan couldn't fight him. *No one* could fight him. This was all just him preening; strutting around to show people how moral and correct he was.

"For the benefit of those watching," Barnabas told him, confirming Lan's fears. "Though not for the reasons you may think. Lan, you are the first in what I assume—jadedly, I admit—will be a long line of people who try to ignore the Queen's laws. They'll give me all sorts of reasons. Some, like King Yoll, will dress it up as divine right. Others, like Jutkelon, will say that no one has any right to interfere in their affairs. You simply thought you could get away with it."

Barnabas shook his head, his expression implacable.

"You can't. That's why I'm here, it's why I exist. You *can't* get away with it. No one can. And you're going to be the first public example of that."

Actually, the carrier was the first example.

Good point, but walking back on that now is going to look ridiculous. Maybe we could just count it as part of the same incident?

Shinigami wished for the umpteenth time that she had eyes to roll.

"Your Queen is also going to fall," Lan promised Barnabas. "You said tyrants always fall. She will fall too!"

Oh no he di-*idn't.*

"I'm going to explain this once, and once only." Barnabas advanced on Lan, his voice dangerously quiet. "Venfaldri Lan, you have disobeyed the laws I follow, which are higher than any of you have known. You disobeyed these laws because you thought you were beyond judgment. *No one* is beyond judgment. My Queen believes that all who desire to make themselves and their lives better should prosper, if their desires harm no one. Those who wish to crush others, however, or use them as you have done? Those people she has *no* mercy for, and neither do I. It is not a tyrant's decree to outlaw slavery, because no matter what words you use or how you hide it behind contracts, that *was* what you were doing—keeping slaves. You were not judged today simply for running a business. You were judged for owning slaves and have been found guilty."

Lan fired, and Barnabas took the bullet and kept advancing. He did not so much as stumble.

"You are going to die, Venfaldri Lan."

Another shot.

By now he really should have figured out those aren't doing anything, Shinigami commented.

The last three shots were made as quickly as Lan could pull the trigger, then he fell to the ground and tried to crawl away—only to have Barnabas haul him upright.

"I suppose it would be too much to hope that you understand your mistake."

Lan's face twisted. "I didn't kiss up to you like Gar did?"

Barnabas's knives raked down Lan's body and he screamed until he died.

"Wrong," Barnabas finished. "But that was what I expected. Your kind never learn."

He looked around as people began to come out of their houses. Ubuara were clustered on the roofs, and Aebura swung down to crouch near Barnabas's feet.

"They're all dead?"

"They are all dead," Barnabas said. He made sure his voice carried. "The ones involved in this, anyway. There may be more. But if there are, we'll catch them, and we'll make them pay, too."

25

"Come see, come see, come see!" Aebura bounded ahead, periodically climbing the sides of buildings and swinging along. She was almost glowing with her exuberance, and her words kept getting lost in the general chitter of her voice. Barnabas could feel the wash of excitement coming off her. It smelled of sunlight and he had a brief, jarring memory of a happy moment in his childhood, bare feet on dirt, summer sunshine and the smell of plants...

He shook his head slightly and continued walking, staring after Aebura when she drew ahead. At his side, Carter was striding with the same sort of excitement, barely in check and tending to ooze out in the form of a wide grin and a bounce in his step. His family would be arriving soon, and he'd been spending the past few days cleaning the bar from top to bottom.

Aebura, who had disappeared into one of the new buildings in the mining town, stuck her head out and bobbed it up and down with impatience.

"Come *see!*"

Barnabas and Carter ducked into the interior of the building.

"Whoa," Carter exclaimed.

"It's...identical." Barnabas looked around.

"Yes! I love the bar in Tethra. That's why this one is the same." Aebura, who was perched on the bar, stroked her fingers over the smooth, freshly-varnished surface. She was radiating happiness.

"Who's going to run it?" Barnabas asked her. "Leiguba?"

"No, I am." She looked even more pleased now.

Carter cleared his throat. "Aebura, I don't mean to be a downer, but running a bar is a lot of work. Trying to run two so far apart? I don't know how you're going to manage."

"I'm not going to run two," she replied. Her excitement had reached a fever pitch in Barnabas's mind and several Ubuara had come to peek in the door, apparently wondering what was going on in here. "You'll run the one in Tethra!"

"*Ah.*" Barnabas smiled as he got it.

Carter gaped at him, then at Aebura. "I'm... I don't know what to... Aebura, are you *sure* you trust me to run your bar for you?"

"It's not *my* bar anymore," she informed him with a pleased flick of her tail. "It's yours. I'm *giving* it to you, Carter Eastbourne."

"It's *mine?*"

"I like you," she explained. "You listen to people, and you help them. You would make a good bartender."

"But...but...."

"Do you not *want* to own the bar?

"No! I mean, yes, I do want to own it! I mean…"

"Well, then it's settled," Aebura told him as if this were the easiest thing in the world. "I want to work here for a while to make this place as nice as possible."

"It really *is* getting much nicer," Barnabas said, sliding onto a bar stool while Carter kept spluttering behind him. "I don't suppose there's any fruit juice?"

Fruit juice? Bobcat would disown you.

It's really good!

Aebura poured a glass and set it on the bar. "I knew you would want some so I had it ready."

"Excellent." Barnabas looked over his shoulder at Carter, who was now staring into the distance and muttering distractedly to himself, then returned to the matter at hand. "So, how are things going with the rebuilding?"

"Very well." Aebura's tail twitched. "Many people have come to help rebuild the living quarters, and some of the original guards are staying to provide security. Not many, just the ones people remember as being nice. *And*," she added, suddenly intent, "you'll never guess what happened! We got all the money in Lan's accounts, and all future ore shipments will pay to our new accounts! We thought it would take years to sort that all out."

"Mmm." Barnabas took a sip of his juice. "I wonder how that happened."

"No one knows." Aebura shrugged her shoulders. "But it really helps with building this place up. We went through the old contracts and standards. He was supposed to be spending a certain amount on the upkeep and he never did!"

Barnabas smiled as Carter came sat down beside them. "Hello. Thought you'd join us, did you? Are you speaking in sentences again?"

Carter just gave him a wide-eyed look and Aebura passed him a glass of juice.

"Did you hear Carter's plans for the bar in Tethra?" she asked Barnabas.

"No plans! There are *no* plans." Carter made a chopping motion with his hand.

"I thought you said—"

"I haven't even really thought about what I'd do here. I'll just play it by ear. But, you know, with good business sense." He gave a deer-in-the-headlights look at Barnabas.

Barnabas smiled back blandly. It wasn't like his mind wasn't broadcasting his intentions, but he'd let Carter keep his illusions.

"So, what's happening with Gar?" Carter asked suddenly.

"Yes." Aebura sat up at once. "What *is* happening with him?"

"Well, he's all healed now." Barnabas rolled his glass on its edge and considered. "I was thinking of taking him on the *Shinigami* with me, if you don't mind. I know you folks had been discussing what should be done with him after the dust settled, so to speak."

Aebura nodded. "Yes, we had."

There were suddenly a lot of Ubuara in the bar. One hopped onto Barnabas's shoulder and leaned on his head.

Not. A. Word.

I need to have someone take pictures of this. I need *to.*

"We discussed it," Aebura said again, looking at the other Ubuara, "and we decided that because Gar went out to confront Lan, thinking he would die, and he *did* get shot and he *would* have died...that counts."

Barnabas blinked. "I see."

"I think I get it," Carter said thoughtfully. "He thought he was paying for it and he made the *choice* to pay for it, and even went through the moment of doing so, so to speak. I could get behind that. This is really good juice," he added.

Barnabas nodded at that.

"So you can take Gar with you if you'd like," Aebura told him, and the other Ubuara nodded. "What will he be doing?"

"I'm not sure." Barnabas had not quite trusted Gar to start his own business just yet. He wanted to watch the male for a while longer. However, Gar also knew some things about the company that effectively controlled High Tortuga for a while and he had good contacts amongst management, many of whom were Luvendi.

Plus, he seemed to know a lot about the various planets and dynamics in this area of space. He was going to be useful.

"Remember to stop back sometimes." Carter smiled. "I know you're all jetting off to do Justice all over the galaxy—"

"Why stop at one galaxy?"

Carter gave him a look. "But you really should check back in and get some juice sometimes."

"Already on the agenda. Plus, I'll have to come see what

you've done with the place." Barnabas looked away from Carter's panicked expression and slid some money across the bar as he stood. "Aebura, a pleasure as always. Carter can get in contact with me if you need anything, so don't hesitate to let him know. Carter, would you like a ride back to Tethra? I hear you have a bar to run."

"Oh! Right." Carter swallowed and hurried out the door after him into the sunlight.

Elisa Eastbourne rolled the stroller over the dusty road between the landing pad and Tethra, and could not help smiling. This place really was exactly as Carter had described—a tiny chaotically-bright city set in the middle of a swamp. The mountains in the distance were crystal clear against the sky, a beautiful sight, and she could smell the street food from here.

"We see Daddy?" Alanna piped up from the stroller. Elisa could just see the glint of her brown hair in the sunlight under the mosquito netting.

"Yes, he said he'd meet us at the landing pad, but he doesn't know we came early. Shhh, it's a surprise." Elisa smiled. "And his assistant—I think it's his assistant— Barnabas said we were supposed to come to his new business."

"We see new city?" Samuel asked.

"Aren't you even a little tired from the trip?"

"No."

She had really walked into that one, Elisa reflected. She was still getting used to the twins being toddlers.

"Well, *I* want a nap," she told them. "So we'll all lie down for a bit once we've seen Daddy again."

Once they reached the city they pushed their way through the crowded streets, and Elisa frowned down one street at a glimpse of a compound that looked totally destroyed. It was, in fact, vaguely smoking. No one seemed worried about it, though, so she supposed it wasn't dangerous.

They found the bar before too much longer and Elisa pushed the stroller inside.

Any plans she'd had for a well-executed surprise went right out the window when the twins unzipped the mosquito netting and piled out to run full-speed across the bar.

"*DADDY!*"

Carter spun around in surprise. "Alanna! Samuel!" He looked up and his smile widened to see his wife. "Elisa," he said, his eyes locked on hers as the twins ran full speed into him and he folded them into his arms. "I missed you! What do you think of Tethra?"

"I love it," Elisa said frankly. She'd always had what her mother and father had called 'a healthy dose of wanderlust,' and none of her family had been surprised when she had signed on with Bethany Anne. This was exactly the sort of place she'd dreamed of visiting. Other people could have their 5-star resorts and fancy dinners. She wanted to see the whole universe.

Carter came to kiss her. "I'm glad you like it," he said, still grinning. "What do you think of the bar?"

"I can't believe you got this up and running in three weeks!"

"Uh, I didn't, actually. It's a long story. I'll introduce you to the former owner at some point."

"Oh, is *that* Barnabas?"

"Barnabas? No, he's Ranger One. Wait, how do you know Barnabas?" Carter stared at her.

"He's how I knew where the bar was, silly! I thought he was your assistant."

"Oh. No." Carter looked around. "In fact, I didn't know he was still—"

"Here?" Barnabas finished. He deposited a crate of glass bottles behind the bar. "Just finishing up a few things, and wanted to stay to meet your family. Elisa, it's so good to meet you." He came over to shake her hand. "Your husband has already *quite* endeared himself to the locals. Now, if you'll excuse me, I really do have to go for now, but I'm sure I'll see you again soon." He slipped around them to the door, then turned back. "Oh, Carter—I brought up one of your crates of Coke. I think the bottling mechanism must be faulty or something. It just doesn't taste...*right.*"

He gave Carter a smile that lingered just a moment too long, then disappeared into the crowds.

"Oh, God," Carter managed to say in a strangled voice.

Back on the *Shinigami*, Barnabas hung his coat neatly on one of the hooks and went to the bridge to look over the schematics and maps Shinigami had printed out. She teased him relentlessly for using paper, but he was still old-fashioned enough to prefer it. There were several more towns already in existence, and a few people trying to establish their own company towns all over the planet. Making High Tortuga safe was going to be a long and involved job.

Barnabas was looking forward to it. He rolled up his sleeves neatly and set to work.

"Shinigami, where's Gar?"

"Doing some research on the planet Luvendan. He believes part of the company may have been based there, and he was as intrigued by my questions on its history as I am."

"Mmm. Well, let me know what you two come up with. On both fronts, I guess." He looked up at one of the cameras. "I don't suppose you have time for a game of chess?"

"Old man, I can play a game of chess *and* do all my work. *You're* the one who needs to make time."

"Oh, really?" Barnabas smiled at her. "Well, then, let's play now, shall we?" He walked over to the board.

"If you insist on getting beaten, I suppose I could oblige you." Shinigami projected a holographic version of herself. "One moment. Why isn't the board coming on?"

"Sometimes you need to turn on electronics to make them work."

"Was that a *threat?*"

"Of course not. Don't be so high-strung." Barnabas thumped the board and smiled as it turned on. "See? It's working now."

"Hrm. I'll have you know I've never had any other troubles with equipment on this ship."

"I wouldn't worry about it." Barnabas settled back in his seat and pressed a tiny button on the side of his watch.

Unbeknownst to Shinigami, a corresponding chip on the bottom of the chess board, installed just a day ago during a 'camera malfunction,' began to run its subroutines. The board Shinigami saw through her cameras would diverge from the board as it actually was.

He hoped this would be an important lesson in perspective and data sources.

Barnabas wondered how long it would take her to realize it. His lips twitched as he nodded to her avatar. "Would you like the first move?"

FINIS

AUTHOR'S NOTES - NATALIE GREY

A couple of years ago I stumbled across the Kurtherian Gambit Universe, and...well, WOW. It's been an amazing time since then—getting to delve into the world with *Bellatrix* and then continue with *Challenges* and the *Trials & Tribulations* series (book 3 is coming out June 21st!).

Those of you who have read *Trials & Tribulations* as well as *Challenges* will remember Barnabas as being very, very sneaky. It's my favorite of his qualities, and one of the most interesting, really. Barnabas is a character of opposites, and often the different sides struggle against each other.

One thing has no opposite, however: his sense of Justice. Barnabas is devoted to doing what is right, and no matter the means, nothing will stand in his way. I love that about him (and I love his friendship with Shinigami).

I want to thank Michael for continuing to allow me to be a part of the KGU, thank the readers for being absolutely amazing, and also to give a special shout-out to the beta team, Kim, Sandy, Jim, and Sam. On the production team, Lynne, Steve, and the JIT group did some above-and-beyond work to help me smooth out a few aspects of lore and make this a nice, clean, typo-free read for everyone else! Furthermore, as you can see, Jeff made a fantastic cover, and Natale did some wonderful behind the scenes work to make this all come together. A round of applause, please!

I can't wait to show you more in Barnabas's world. Happy reading!

-Nat

AUTHOR NOTES - MICHAEL ANDERLE

MAY 21ST, 2018

First, THANK YOU for not only reading this story, but these notes as well!

With this book I have accomplished a goal (or maybe I should call it a desire more than a goal) with Natalie (whose real name is <redacted>.) I was looking at having something ghost-written, sort of.

You see, I was speaking with Natalie over a year ago, I think, to see if she wanted to either take income for writing the book or collaboration income, and at the time, for personal reasons, she chose payment up front. I can't blame her, since she had NO idea at the time whether this Universe would make her any money, and she was a big piece of the income for her family.

However, I didn't let *that* deter me.

Nope, I chose to share with Natalie the sales figures for the books for three to four months so that she could (I hoped, *boy* did I hope) make a choice to come back into the Kurtherian Gambit Universe as a collaborator. Plus, I setup a pen name for her so that she could get name recognition when the time was right to come back into the Universe and play again.

She might have written these stories a little faster, but she had a baby in the middle of all of this. I guess that's a pretty good reason to slow down the writing just a little.

Who types and writes books when they are working with babies? Perhaps Natalie can, but I know I can't.

When she came back "into the fold" (like the lost sheep I pretend she was...not that she was...in fact she released a whole trilogy as Natalie Grey, but let me pretend, ok?) Anyway, when Natalie came back and we spoke, I was mentioning that I had the big 'explosion' of character directions that was going to take place as Bethany Anne's last book in The Kurtherian Gambit occurred and where I wanted to take Barnabas.

Basically "out there!"

Somewhere.

I pitched her doing THIS series and her voice lit up (no, really. If you ever speak with Natalie you CAN hear her voice light up over the phone, I promise!) Her style is naturally INTENSE, so Barnabas being a bit of a hardass and yet having to figure out how to work with an AI who was imprinted with Baba Yaga seemed JUST like the type of story she would do well with.

And now *you* have this first story in your hands.

I hope you enjoyed it, and if you would like to read any of Natalie's OTHER stories, just go here:

https://www.amazon.com/Natalie-Grey/e/B01MYG7K8P/

If you would like to see other Kurtherian Gambit books try this link:

Kurtherian Gambit Books at Amazon

As always, every author is boosted by your support in reading our books, reviewing our books, and when you talk with fellow book lovers, telling them about your favorite authors (and BOOKS!) ;-)

Ad Aeternitatem and have a *blessed* day,

Michael Anderle

BOOKS BY NATALIE GREY

Shadows of Magic

Bound Sorcery

Blood Sorcery

Bright Sorcery

Set in the Kurtherian Gambit Universe

Bellatrix

Challenges

Risk Be Damned

Damned to Hell

Vigilante

Writing as Moira Katson

Shadowborn

Shadowforged

Shadow's End

Daughter of Ashes

Mahalia

CONNECT WITH THE AUTHORS

Natalie Grey Social

Email List

https://landing.mailerlite.com/webforms/landing/w0k9j4

Follow Natalie on Amazon

https://www.amazon.com/Natalie-Grey/e/B01MYG7K8P/

Facebook

https://www.facebook.com/Natalie-Grey-393234677682987/

Michael Anderle Social
Website:
http://www.lmbpn.com

Email List:
http://lmbpn.com/email/

Facebook Here:
https://www.facebook.com/OriceranUniverse/

https://www.facebook.com/

TheKurtherianGambitBooks/